"I Have Better Things To Do With My Time Than Entertain You For The Next Thirty Days."

She immediately saw red. "Entertain me? I guess you're assuming if we do decide to live together for the next month it will be here, at your place."

He shrugged as if to ease the tension in his shoulders and said, "Of course."

She frowned. He sounded so sure and confident. "Wrong," she said, taking great joy in bursting his bubble.

His eyes narrowed into
glare at her. "An ... 'll
stay?"

She glared back.
where *you'll* stay. ... and if
you want to fulfill ... the decree you will,
too!"

Dear Reader,

When I introduced the Westmoreland triplets in *Stone Cold Surrender* (Silhouette Desire #1601), I was already imagining a love interest for each of them. Getting Casey together with McKinnon Quinn was a definite yes. Then I had to wonder about Clint and Cole.

This is Clint Westmoreland's story. I decided to place him in a no-win situation by using my infamous *what if? What if* while a Texas Ranger he married his partner, Alyssa Bartley, to infiltrate an illegal adoption ring, and then five years later he discovered the marriage had never been annulled? And *what if* he discovered that before the marriage could be annulled they had to live together for thirty days?

Now with those issues clearly established—not to mention *what if* we throw in a good dose of sexual attraction that neither of them can kick—it's time for me to work my magic and transform a man who definitely doesn't have love and marriage on his mind into a definite goner.

I hope all of you enjoy reading Clint and Alyssa's story as much as I enjoyed writing it.

Happy reading!

Brenda Jackson

BRENDA JACKSON

TAMING CLINT WESTMORELAND

Published by Silhouette Books
America's Publisher of Contemporary Romance

ISBN-13: 978-0-373-76850-9
ISBN-10: 0-373-76850-8

TAMING CLINT WESTMORELAND

This edition published by arrangement with Harlequin Books S.A.

Visit Silhouette Books at www.eHarlequin.com

Printed in U.S.A.

Recent books by Brenda Jackson

Silhouette Desire

**The Chase Is On* #1690
**The Durango Affair* #1727
**Ian's Ultimate Gamble* #1756
**Seduction, Westmoreland Style* #1778
Stranded with the Tempting Stranger #1825
**Spencer's Forbidden Passion* #1838
**Taming Clint Westmoreland* #1850

*Westmoreland family titles

Kimani Romance

Solid Soul #1
Night Heat #9
Risky Pleasures #37
In Bed with the Boss #53

BRENDA JACKSON

is a die "heart" romantic who married her childhood sweetheart and still proudly wears the going steady ring he gave her when she was fifteen. Because she's always believed in the power of love, Brenda's stories always have happy endings. In her real-life love story, Brenda and her husband of thirty-three years live in Jacksonville, Florida, and have two sons.

A *USA TODAY* bestselling author, Brenda divides her time between family, writing and working in management at a major insurance company. You can write Brenda at P.O. Box 28267, Jacksonville, FL 32226, by e-mail at WriterBJackson@aol.com or visit her Web site at www.brendajackson.net.

ACKNOWLEDGMENTS

To Gerald Jackson, Sr., the love of my life.

To all my readers who have made the Westmorelands a very special family in their hearts. This book is for you!

To my Heavenly Father. How Great Thou Are.

Better a meal of vegetables where there is love
than a fattened calf with hatred.
—*Proverbs* 15:17

One

Clint Westmoreland glanced around the airport and silently cursed. It was the middle of the day, he had a ton of work to do back at his ranch and here he stood waiting to meet a wife he hadn't known he'd had until a few days ago.

His chest tightened as he inwardly fumed, recalling the contents of the letter he'd received from the Texas State Bureau of Investigations. He'd learned from the letter that when he'd gotten married while working on an undercover sting operation five years ago as a Texas Ranger, the marriage had never been nullified by the agency. That meant that he and Alyssa Barkley, the woman who had been his female partner, were still legally married.

The thought of being married, legally or otherwise, sent a chill down his spine, and the sooner he and Alyssa could meet and get the marriage annulled the better. She had received a similar letter and a few days ago they had spoken on the phone. She, too, was upset about the bureau's monumental screwup and had agreed to fly to Austin to get the matter resolved immediately.

He glanced at his watch thinking time was being wasted. It was the first of February and he had a shipment of wild horses due any day and needed to get things ready at the ranch for their arrival.

When he had announced at his cousin Ian's wedding last June that he would be leaving the Rangers after ten years, his cousin Durango and his brother-in-law, McKinnon Quinn, had invited him to join their Montana-based, million-dollar horse-breeding business. They wanted him to expand their company into Texas. Clint would run the Texas operations and become a partner in the business. His main focus would be taming and training wild horses.

He had accepted their offer and hadn't regretted a day of doing so. So to his way of thinking, at this moment he had more important things he should be concentrating on. Like making sure his horse-taming business stayed successful.

He glanced at his watch again and then looked around wondering if he would recognize Alyssa when he saw her. It had been five years and the only thing he could recall about her was that she'd been young, right out of college with a degree in criminal justice. The two of them had been together less than a week. That was all the time it had taken to play the part of a young married couple who desperately wanted to adopt a baby—illegally.

She had played the part of a despairing, wannabe mother pretty convincingly. So much in fact that a sting operation everyone had assumed would take a couple of weeks to pull off had ended after the first week. Afterward, he had been sent on another assignment. From what he'd heard, she had turned in her resignation after deciding being a Texas Ranger wasn't what she wanted to devote her life to doing after all.

He had no idea what she'd done since then, as their phone conversation had been brief and he hadn't been inclined to even ask. He wanted the issue of their being married dealt with so they could both get on with their lives. She should be about twenty-seven now, he thought. On the phone, she'd said she was still single. Actually, he'd been surprised that she hadn't gotten married or something.

The sound of high heels clicking on the ceramic tile floor made him glance at the woman strolling in his direction. He blinked. If the woman was Alyssa, she had certainly gone through one hell of a transformation. Although she'd been far from a plain Jane before, there hadn't been anything about her to make him want to take a second look…until now.

He could definitely see her on the cover of some sexy magazine. And it was apparent that he wasn't the only person who thought so, judging by the blatant male attention she was getting. One man had the nerve to stop walking, stand in the middle of the walkway as if he were glued to the spot and openly stare at her.

Clint cut the spectator a fierce frown, which made the man quickly turn and continue walking. Then Clint felt angry with himself for momentarily losing his senses to play the part of a jealous husband, until he remembered that legally he *was* Alyssa's husband. So he had a right to get jealous if he wanted to…if that rationale at the moment made any damn sense, which it probably didn't.

He shook his head remembering how men used to have the same reaction to his sister, Casey, and he hadn't liked it then, either. For some reason he liked it even less now.

Alyssa was closer and the first thing he thought, besides the fact she was a looker, was that she certainly knew how to wear a pair of jeans. Her hips swayed with each step she took and impossible as it might seem, although he hadn't felt an attraction to her five years ago, he was definitely feeling some strong vibes now.

He was so absorbed in checking her out that it hadn't occurred to him just how close she was until she came to a stop directly in front of him, up close and personal and all in his space. Now he saw everything. The dark eyes, long lashes, high cheekbones, full lips, head of curly copper-colored hair and a gorgeous medium-brown face.

And he heard the sexy voice that went along with those features when she spoke and said, "Hello, Clint. I'm here."

She most certainly was!

* * *

He hasn't changed, Alyssa thought as she struggled to keep up with his brisk stride as they walked together out of the airport to the parking lot. At six-four he was a lot taller than her five-eight height, and the black Stetson he wore on his head was still very much a part of his wardrobe.

But she would admit that his face had matured in ways that only a woman who had concentrated on it years before could notice. The first time they'd met she thought he was more handsome than any man had a right to be, and now at thirty-two he was even more so. Even then she had concluded that the perfection of his features was due to the cool, arrogant lines that underscored his eyes and the dimples that set boldly in his cheeks—regardless of whether he smiled or not.

Then there were his chin and jaw that seemed to have been carved flawlessly, not to mention full lips that were, in her opinion, way too perfect to belong to any man. To say he hadn't made quite an impression on a fresh-out-of-college, twenty-two-year-old virgin was an understatement. The one thing she wouldn't forget was that she'd had one hell of a crush on him, just like so many other women who'd worked for the bureau.

"My truck is parked over there," he said.

His words intruded into her thoughts and she glanced up and met his gaze. "Are we going straight to the Rangers' headquarters?" she asked, trying not to make it so obvious that she was studying his lips.

Those lips were what had drawn her to him from the

first. He'd been a man of few words, but his lips, whenever they had moved, had always been worth the wait. They demanded attention. And she would even go so far to say, demanded a plan of action that tempted you to taste them. Dreaming of kissing him had been something she'd done often.

Needless to say, she had been the envy of several female Rangers when she'd been the one chosen to work with him on that assignment. He was considered a private person and she seriously doubted that at the time he'd been aware of just how many women had lusted after him, or made him a constant participant in their fantasies.

"Yes, we can go straight there," he answered, breaking into the middle of her thoughts. "I figure it shouldn't take long to do what needs to be done. Hopefully no more than an hour," he said.

She was suddenly tempted to stop walking, place her hand on his arm and lean up on tiptoes and go ahead and boldly steal a kiss. The very thought made her heart rate accelerate.

Inhaling, she tried concentrating on what he'd said. She, too, hoped that what needed to be done wouldn't take more than an hour. If she spent much more time with this man, Alyssa was certain she would lose her mind. Besides, she hadn't brought any luggage, just an overnight bag. After they took care of matters, she would check into a hotel for the night and fly back to Waco in the morning.

"So, how have you been, Alyssa?"

She glanced over at him. She knew he was trying to

be cordial so she smiled accordingly, while thinking another thing he'd still retained over the years was that deep, sexy voice. "I've been doing fine, Clint. And you?"

"I can't complain."

She figured he couldn't if what she'd heard from the few friends she still had with the bureau was true. No longer a Ranger, Clint now operated a horse-breeding ranch on the outskirts of Austin on over three hundred acres of land. It was a ranch he had inherited from a close relative. And according to her sources, the horse-breeding business was doing quite well. Although she was curious as to why he had left the force, she really didn't feel comfortable enough with Clint to ask him about it. She would have sworn he'd make a career of it.

Deciding it was none of her business, she thought of something that was and said, "I can't believe the bureau would make such a mistake. The nerve of them sending that letter saying we're married."

They had reached his truck and he shrugged massive shoulders when he opened the truck door for her. "I couldn't believe it at first myself. I guess it's a good thing neither of us ever took a notion to marry."

She decided not to tell him that she *had* taken a notion a couple of years ago, and had come as close as the day of her wedding before finding out what a weasel she'd been engaged to. To this day Kevin Brady hadn't forgiven her for leaving him standing at the altar. But then she hadn't forgiven him for sleeping with her cousin Kim a week before the wedding.

From the corner of her eye she could tell that Clint

was looking at her as she slid into the smooth leather seat and couldn't help wondering if he could see the heat that had risen in her cheeks denoting there was something she wasn't telling him.

"You look different than before," he said, as he casually leaned against the truck's open door.

She threw him a sharp glance at his comment and wondered if she should take what he'd said as a compliment or an insult. She decided to probe further and asked, "In what way?"

"Different."

A smile touched her cheeks. He was still a man of few words. "I am different," she admitted.

"In what way?"

She chuckled. Now he was the one asking that question. "I live my life the way I want and not the way others think that I should."

"Is that what you were doing five years ago?"

"Yes." And she figured he didn't need to know any more than that. He must have thought so, as well, because he closed the door and crossed in front of the truck to the driver's side without inquiring further.

"It will be lunchtime in a little while," he said after easing onto the seat and closing the door shut. "Do you want to stop somewhere and grab a bite to eat before we meet with Hightower?"

Lester Hightower had been the senior captain in charge of field operations when they had done that undercover assignment five years ago. "No, I prefer that we meet with Hightower as soon as possible," she said.

He lifted a brow as he glanced over at her. "Maybe I spoke too soon earlier. If you hadn't taken a notion to get married before should I assume you might be considering such a move now?"

She stared over at him and he did something she hadn't expected. He smiled. And immediately she tried to ignore the heat that touched her body when the corners of his lips curved. "No, you can't assume that. I just don't like surprises and getting that letter was definitely a surprise."

He nodded as he broke eye contact to start the engine. "Yes, but it's one we shouldn't have a problem fixing."

"I hope you're right."

He glanced back over at her as he backed out of the parking space. "Of course I'm right. You'll see."

"What the hell do you mean we can't get the marriage annulled?" Clint all but roared. He could not have been more shocked with what Hightower had just said.

This was the first time, in all his twelve years of knowing the man, that Clint had raised his voice to his former boss. Of course, if he'd done such a thing while still a Ranger, he would have been reprimanded severely. But Hightower was no longer his superior, and Clint felt entitled to a straight answer from the man.

He glanced over at Alyssa. She had gotten out of her chair and was leaning against the closed door. He could tell from her not-too-happy expression that she wanted answers, as well. He frowned thinking he had known the exact moment she had moved from the chair to stand by the door. He had been listening to Hightower, but at the same time he'd been very much aware of her. An uncomfortable sensation slid up his spine. He hadn't been this fully aware of a woman in a long time.

"New procedures are in place, Westmoreland," Clint heard Hightower say. "I don't like them nor do I understand them. And I agree the one in your particular situation doesn't make sense because proper procedures weren't followed. But there's nothing else I can tell you. We tried rectifying our mistake by immediately filing for an annulment on your and Barkley's behalf, but since so much time has passed and because the two of you no longer work for the agency, the State is dragging their tail in acknowledging that your marriage is not a real one."

"You're right, that doesn't make any sense," Alyssa said sharply. "Clint and I have never lived under the same roof. For heaven's sake, the marriage was never consummated, so that in itself should be grounds to grant an annulment."

"And under normal circumstances, it would be, but the new person in charge of that department, a woman by the name of Margaret Toner, thinks otherwise. From what I understand, Toner has been married for over forty years and takes the institution of marriage seriously. We might not like it or understand her reasoning, but for now we have to abide by it."

"Like hell!" Clint bit out, not believing what he was hearing.

"Like hell or heaven, it doesn't matter," Hightower

said, throwing a document on the desk. "Thirty days. Toner has agreed to grant an annulment to your and Barkley's marriage in thirty days."

Neither Clint nor Alyssa said anything for a long moment, both figuring it was best not to, otherwise they would say the wrong thing. Instead they decided to keep the anger they felt inside. But then finally, as if accepting the finality of their situation, Alyssa spoke. "I don't like it, Hightower, but if nothing can be done about it for thirty days, there's little Clint and I can do. It's been five years without me even knowing I was a married woman, so I guess another thirty days won't kill me," she said, glancing over at Clint.

He frowned. Although it wouldn't kill him, either, he didn't like it one damn bit. He enjoyed being a bachelor although unlike his brother, Cole, he'd never earned the reputation of being a ladies's man. But Alyssa was right, they had been married five years without either of them knowing it, so another thirty days would not make or break them. There was nothing in his life that would be changing.

"Fine," he all but snapped. "Like Alyssa, I'll deal with it for thirty more days."

"There's one more thing," Hightower hesitated a few moments before saying.

Clint's frown deepened. He had worked with the man long enough to detect something in his voice, something Clint figured he wouldn't like. Evidently, Alyssa picked up on it, as well, and moved away from the door to come and stand beside him.

"What other thing?" Clint asked.

Hightower shrugged massive shoulders nervously. "Not sure how the two of you are going to feel about it, but Toner wouldn't back down or change her mind about it."

"About what?" Clint asked in an agitated voice.

Hightower looked at him and then at Alyssa. "In order for the marriage to get annulled after the thirty days, there is something the two of you must do."

Clint felt his heart turn over. He felt another strange sensation slither up his spine. He knew, without a doubt, that he wouldn't like whatever Hightower was about to say. "And just what does Toner wants us to do?" he asked, trying to keep his voice calm.

Hightower cleared his throat and then said, "She has mandated that during those thirty days the two of you live under the same roof."

Two

It didn't take much to figure out that Clint Westmoreland was one angry man, Alyssa thought, glancing over at him. They had left Hightower's office over twenty minutes ago, and now Clint was driving her to a place where she assumed they would grab a bite to eat. But he had yet to say one word to her. Not one. However, that didn't take into consideration the number of times he'd mumbled the word *damn* under his breath.

Sighing deeply, she decided to brave the icy waters and said, "Surely there's something we can do."

He speared her with a look that could probably freeze boiling water and his mouth was set in a grim line. However, to her his lips still looked as delectable as a slice of key lime pie. "You heard what he said, Alyssa.

We can try to appeal, but if we're not successful we will still have to do the thirty days, which will only delay things," he said.

Do the thirty days. He'd made it sound like a jail sentence. And since he would have to share the same roof with her, she wasn't sure she particularly liked his attitude. She didn't like what Hightower had said any more than he did, but there was no reason to get rude about it.

"Look," she said. "I don't like this any more than you do, but if we can't change things then we need to do what Toner is requiring and—"

"The hell I will," he said almost in a growl when he looked back at her. He had pulled into the parking lot of a restaurant and had brought his truck to a stop. "I have more to do with my time for the next thirty days than entertain you."

She immediately saw red. "Entertain me? From saying that, I guess you're assuming if we do decide to live together for the next thirty days it will be here at your place."

He shrugged as if to ease the tension in his shoulders and said, "Of course."

She frowned. He sounded so sure and confident. She would take joy in bursting his bubble. "Wrong. I have no intention of staying here in Austin with you."

His eyes narrowed into slits as he continued to glare at her. "And just where do you assume you'll stay?"

She glared back. "It's not where I'll stay but where you'll stay. I'm returning to Waco and if you want to fulfill the terms of Toner's decree you will, too."

If she thought he was mad before then it was quite obvious he was madder now. “Look, lady. I have a ranch to run and I won’t be doing it from Waco.”

“You’re not the only one who owns a business, Clint. I’m not going to drop everything that’s going on in my life just to come out here to live with you.”

“And neither will I drop everything I’ve got going on here to move to Waco, even temporarily. That’s as stupid as stupid can get.”

She had to agree with him there, but still that didn’t solve their problem. According to Hightower, they needed to live under the same roof for thirty days, which meant that one of them had to compromise. But she didn’t feel it should be her and evidently he didn’t think it should be him, either. “Okay, you don’t want to move to Waco and I don’t want to move here, so what do you suggest we do to get that annulment?” she asked him.

He pulled his key out of the truck’s ignition and said, “I don’t know, but what I do know is that I think better on a full stomach.” He opened the door to get out. “Right now I suggest that we get something to eat.”

By the time the waitress had taken their order, Clint was convinced that somebody up there didn’t like him. If they did, they would not have dumped Alyssa Barkley in his lap. The woman was too much of a tempting package and someone he didn’t have time to deal with. The thought of her living under his roof, or for that matter, him living under hers, was too much too imagine. But he had been a Ranger long enough to know just how tangled red tape could get. Someone had screwed up. Otherwise they wouldn't still be married—at least on paper. As she'd told Hightower, the marriage hadn't even been consummated. It had been an assignment, nothing more.

"You're a triplet, right?"

He glanced at her over the rim of his glass. "Yes. How do you know that?"

She shrugged. "It was common knowledge among the Rangers. I met your brother, Cole, once. He was nice. I also heard you have a sister."

"I do," he said, thinking about Casey, who had gotten married a few months ago. "If you go by order of birth, then I'm the oldest, then Cole and last Casey."

"Is Cole still a Texas Ranger?"

He figured she must feel a little more relaxed to be asking so many questions. "Yes, he is."

He didn't know her well enough to reveal that Cole's days with the Rangers were numbered. Like him, Cole planned to go out on early retirement; however, Cole hadn't decided what he'd do after leaving the force. Clint wasn't even sure if Cole planned to stay in Texas. His brother might take a notion to move to Montana like Casey had done to be near their father. The father the three of them thought was dead until a few years ago.

He took a sip of his coffee. In a way he knew what Alyssa was doing. She was trying to get his mind off the gigantic problem that was looming over their heads. But the bottom line was that they needed to talk about it and make some decisions. "Okay, Alyssa, getting back to our dilemma. What about you? Do you have any suggestions?"

She took a sip of her coffee and smiled before saying, "I guess I could go back to Waco and you remain here and forget we ever found out we were married and leave things as they are. As I said earlier, marriage isn't in my future anytime soon. What about yours?"

"Not in mine, either, but still, having a wife isn't something I can forget about," he said. *Several things could happen later to make him remember he was a married man.*

For example, what would happen if she decided, as his wife, that she was entitled to half of everything he owned? His partnership with his cousin and brother-in-law was going extremely well. Not saying that she would, but he couldn't take any chances. He had bought out Casey's and Cole's shares of the ranch and now it was totally his. The last thing he would tolerate was a "wife" staking a claim on anything that had his name on it.

And then there was the other reason he wouldn't be able to forget he had a wife. She was too damn pretty. Her features were too striking and her body was too well-stacked. Even now sitting across from her at the table he could feel his temperature rise. Since he figured she hadn't gotten that way overnight, he wondered how he had missed noticing how good she looked five years ago. The only excuse he could come up with was that at the time he'd been too heavily involved with Chantelle and only had eyes for one woman. Too bad Chantelle hadn't had eyes for just one man.

"There has to be a way out of this," she said, interrupting his thoughts with a disgusted look on her face. Disgusted or otherwise, her frustration didn't downplay how full and firm her lips were, or how her eyes were so dark they reminded him of a raven's wing. He wondered if her copper-brown hair was her natural color and he felt a tug in his gut when he thought of the one way he could easily find out. He shifted in his seat. His jeans suddenly felt a little too tight, especially in the area of his zipper.

Evidently she was waiting for him to respond, because her dark eyes were staring at him. He leaned back in his chair. "There is a way. We just have to think of it."

Alyssa could feel Clint checking her out the same way she was checking him out, which only solidified her belief that living under the same roof with him wouldn't work. There was a strong sexual attraction between them, she could feel it. The thought that she drew his interest was something she couldn't ignore. Nor was it something for her to lose any sleep over. Plenty of women probably drew his attention. He was a man wasn't he? Hadn't Uncle Jessie explained after finding out what Kim and Kevin had done that when it came to women all men were weak? They often made decisions with the "wrong head." Of course, he couldn't come up with an excuse for Kim's behavior because she was his daughter.

"What sort of business do you own?"

She glanced up from studying the contents in her coffee cup to stare into Clint's cool, dark eyes. "I design Web sites."

"Oh."

She frowned. He'd said it as though he considered her profession of no importance. Granted it wasn't a mega-million-dollar operation like she'd heard he owned but it was hers; one she'd started a few years ago with all the money she had. She enjoyed her work and was proud of the way she'd built up her company. She had a very nice clientele who depended on her to keep their businesses in the forefront of the cyberspace market. Over the years she had won numerous awards for her Web site designs.

"For your information I own a very successful business," she said, glaring at him.

He glared back. "I don't recall saying you didn't."

No, he hadn't. But still, she really didn't care much for his attitude. "Look, Clint. You're agitated about this whole thing and so am I. I think the best thing for us to do is sleep on it. Maybe we'll have answers in the morning."

"Fine. I noticed you only brought an overnight bag," he said, leaning back in his chair.

"Yes. I thought that ending our marriage wouldn't take more than a day at the most. I planned to fly home in the morning."

"You're welcome to stay at my place tonight. I have plenty of room."

She appreciated the invitation but didn't think it was a good idea. "Thanks, but I prefer staying at a hotel."

"Suit yourself," he said, easing back up to the table when their waitress placed a plate full of food in front of him. Alyssa watched him dig in. He'd said he could think better on a full stomach, but was he really going to eat all that? She couldn't imagine him eating such hefty meals as the norm, especially since he had such a well-built body that was all muscle and no fat.

"Why are you staring at my plate?"

She shrugged. "That's a lot of food," she said when the waitress placed a sandwich and bowl of soup in front of her.

He laughed. "I'm still growing. Besides, I need all this to keep my strength up. What I do around the ranch is hard work."

"And what exactly do you do?"

He smiled over at her. "I'm a horse tamer. I have some of my men stationed out in Nevada. They capture wild horses then ship them to my ranch for me to tame. Once that's done, I ship them to Montana. My cousin and brother-in-law own a horse-breeding company. My sister works for them as a trainer."

"Sounds like a family affair."

"It is."

Alyssa intentionally kept her head lowered as she ate her sandwich and soup. She didn't want to risk looking head-on into Clint's eyes again. Each time she did so made every cell in her body vibrate.

"I'm thinking of getting one of those."

She raised her head and gazed at him, trying not to zero in on his handsome features, while at the same time ignoring the sensations that flowed through her. "Getting one of what?"

"A Web site."

She lifted a brow. "You don't have one already?"

"No."

"Why not?"

"Why would I?"

"Mainly to promote your business."

"Don't have to. Durango and McKinnon are in charge of bringing in the customers. We have a private clientele."

"Oh. Who are Durango and McKinnon?"

He wiped his mouth with a napkin before answering. "Durango is my cousin and McKinnon is married to my sister, Casey. They are my partners and the ones who started the horse-breeding company. Now it has grown to include horse training and horse taming," he said.

She nodded. "If you did just fine without a Web site before, then why are you thinking about getting one now?"

He actually looked like he was tired of answering her questions. His tone indicated that he was only answering her in an attempt to be polite. "Because of the foundation I recently started."

"What foundation?"

"The Sid Roberts Foundation." And as if he was preparing for her next question, he said, "He was my uncle."

Her eyes widened. "Sid Roberts? The Sid Roberts? Was your uncle?" she asked incredulously.

"Yes," he responded, seemingly again with barely

tolerant patience. And then as if he'd had enough of her questions he said, "Why don't you finish eating. Your soup is getting cold."

At least he had gotten her to stop talking, Clint thought, taking a sip of his coffee. Although he noticed what she was eating wasn't much. He'd thought Casey was the only person who considered soup and a sandwich a full-course meal.

Clint leaned back in his chair. The food was great and he was full, so now he could think. Yet he was far from having an answer to their problem. Part of him wanted to start the appeal process and see what would happen. But if the appeal failed, they would have to do the thirty days anyway.

"You didn't say why you are establishing a foundation for your uncle."

He glanced over at her. "Didn't I?" he asked tersely. He couldn't recall her being this chatty before. In fact, he remembered her as a mousy young woman who didn't seem to have the fortitude for her job as a Ranger. Although truth be told, he would be the first to give her an A for her acting abilities during their assignment together.

He couldn't help noticing how the sunlight shining through the window hit her hair at an angle that gave the copper strands a golden tint. He felt a sudden tingling sensation right smack in his gut. He didn't like the feeling. Since becoming partners with Durango and

McKinnon nine months ago, he had placed his social life—and women—on hold.

"No, you didn't," she said, breaking into his thoughts and seemingly not the least put off by his cool tone.

He didn't say anything for a while and then asked, "What do you know about Sid Roberts?"

She smiled. "Only what's in the history books, as well as what my grandfather shared with me."

He lifted a brow. "Your grandfather?"

"Yes, he was a huge Sid Roberts fan and even claimed to being a part of the rodeo circuit with him at one time. I know Mr. Roberts was a legend in his day. First as a rodeo star then as a renowned horse trainer."

"Uncle Sid loved horses and passed that love on to me, my brother and sister. In my uncle's memory, we have dedicated over three thousand acres of land on the south ridge of my property as a reserve. A great number of the wild horses that are being shipped to me are being turned loose to roam free here."

"Why go to the trouble of relocating them here? Why not leave them in Nevada and let them run free there?"

He frowned. "Mainly because wild horses are taking up land that's now needed for public use. Legislation is being considered that will allow for so many of them to be destroyed each year. Many of these wild horses are getting slaughtered for pet food."

"That's awful," she murmured and he knew she was deliberately lowering her voice to keep out the anger she felt. It was the same with him every time he thought about it.

"Yes, it is. So I've established the foundation as a

way to save as many of the wild horses as I can by bringing them here."

He felt they had gotten off track, and had put on the back burner the subject they really needed to be discussing. "So what are we going to do, Alyssa, about our marriage?"

She frowned. "You make it sound like a real one when it's not."

"Then tell that to Toner. And maybe it's time to accept that regardless of where we want to place the blame, legally we are man and wife."

Alyssa opened her mouth to deny what he said, but couldn't. He was right. They could sit and blame others but that wouldn't solve their problem. "Okay, you have a full stomach, what do you suggest?"

"You're not going to like it."

"Probably not if it's what I'm thinking."

He sighed deeply. "Do we have a choice?"

She knew they didn't but still… "There has to be another way."

"According to Hightower, there isn't. You heard him for yourself."

"I say let's fight it."

"And I say let's just do what we have to do and get it over with."

She nibbled on her bottom lip. "Fine, but there's still the issue of where we'll stay. Here or Waco." Each knew how the other felt on the subject. Alyssa knew she was being hard-nosed. To handle his business properly, he would have to be on his ranch, whereas she could operate just about anywhere, as long as she had her computer and server.

"Alyssa?"

She glanced up at him. "Yes?"

"I'm sure you prefer handling your business from Waco, but is there any reason you can't do it here if I help get things set up for you?" he asked, evidently thinking along the same lines as she had earlier.

She decided to be honest with him. "No."

"All right. Then will you?" he asked. "My ranch isn't all that bad. It's pretty nice actually. And with the hours I work, I'd barely be home most of the time so it will be as if you have the place to yourself. I won't be underfoot."

She tilted her head to study him. In other words they really wouldn't be under the same roof for thirty days—at least not all the time. In a way, she would prefer it that way. Being around Clint 24/7 would be too hard to handle. But she knew he was right. They had to do something and since it was easier for her to make the change why sweat it. That didn't mean she had to like it. At least the two of them were working together and doing what needed to be done to get their lives back on track and end what had been the agency's screwup and not theirs. But still…

"What about a steady girlfriend?" she decided to ask.

"Don't have one, steady or otherwise. Don't have the time."

She lifted a brow. *When did men stop making the time for women?* She thought they lived for intimacy.

"What about you?" he asked her. "Is there a steady man in your life?"

She thought about the occasional calls she got from Kevin as he tried to make a comeback, as if she didn't know that he and Kim were still messing around with each other. Kim took pleasure in making comments every once in a while to let her know she and Kevin were still seeing each other now and then. "No, like you, I don't have the time."

He nodded. "So, there's really nothing holding us back to do what we need to do to get the matter resolved," he said.

If only it were that simple, she wanted to say. Instead she said, "I need to sleep on it." She preferred not to make a decision right then.

"Okay. In that case would you mind doing your sleeping at the ranch?" Clint asked. "That way, you can check out the place to see if it will work for you."

She'd rather not stay at his ranch tonight but what he'd said made sense. She was used to living in the city. She wasn't sure how she would handle being out in such a rural setting. "Okay, Clint. I'll spend the night at your ranch and will give you my decision about things in the morning."

He tilted his head and looked at her. "I can't ask for any more than that."

Three

"Can you ride a horse?"

Alyssa glanced over at Clint. Sunlight streaming in through the windshield seemed to highlight his features. It had been bad enough sitting across from him at the diner trying to eat. Now they were back in the close quarters of his truck and everything male about him was out in the forefront again. She moved her gaze from his face to the strong, sturdy hands that were gripping the steering wheel, and then lower to his lap where the denim of his jeans stretched tight across muscular thighs.

"Alyssa?"

She nearly jumped when he said her name again, reminding her that she hadn't answered his question. "Yes and no."

He glanced over at her and frowned. "You either can or you can't."

"Not necessarily. There's another option—can and don't. Yes, I can ride a horse, but I choose not to."

He gave her a strange look. "Is there a reason why?"

"Yes. What if I say that horses don't like me?"

He gave a half laugh. "Then I'd say that if you feel that way it means you haven't developed your own personal technique of dealing with them. A horse can detect a lot from people. Whether you're too aggressive, too nice, sometimes both. A horse is the most easy-going animal that I know of."

"Yeah, you would say that since you tame them," she said, glancing out the truck window and thinking how beautiful the land was getting the farther they got away from the city.

"I'd say it even if I didn't tame them. If you stay at the ranch I guarantee you will develop a liking for horses."

"I never said I didn't like them, Clint. It's just I've been thrown off one too many times to suit my fancy. I know when to give in and quit."

He chuckled. "I don't. And if I stopped riding based on the number of times I've been thrown, I would have given up riding years ago. That's part of it. Learning to ride with the intent of staying on."

Alyssa heard what he was saying but it wouldn't change her mind. The truck had come to a stop and she glanced over at Clint. He was staring at her in a way that had her pulse racing, was making her feel breathless. A brazen image formed in her mind. "What?" she asked in a low voice.

It was as if that one single word made him realize that he'd been staring and when the truck began moving again, he muttered, "Nothing."

It was there on the tip of Alyssa's tongue to say yes, it had been something and she had felt it, too, in the cozy space surrounding them. As she glanced back out the window, she thought that living on a ranch with him wouldn't be easy. The only good thing was that he'd said he would be gone most of the time. That was good to know for her peace of mind.

"Will your family have a problem with it?"

She glanced back over at him. He was staring straight ahead and she thought that was good. Every time he looked at her, sensations she hadn't felt in a long time, or ever, seemed to unleash inside of her. "A problem with what?" she asked, thinking she liked the sound of his voice a little too much.

"Living with me for a while at the ranch. That is if you decide to do it."

Alyssa sighed. There was no need to go into any details that certain members of her family wouldn't care if she left Waco for good. It was all too complicated to get into and too personal to explain. That was the only good thing about the thirty days. Time away from Waco was probably what she needed. Ruining her wedding day hadn't been enough for Kim. She was determined to sabotage any decent thing that came into Alyssa's life.

"No, they wouldn't have a problem with it," she finally answered. "What about your folks?"

He glanced over at her and smiled and that single smile ignited a torch within her. She actually felt heat flowing through her body. "My family is fine with whatever I do. My brother, sister and I are extremely close but we know when to give each other space and when to mind our own business." He then chuckled and the sound raked across her skin in a sensuous sort of way.

"Okay, I admit when it came to Casey, Cole and I never did mind our own business. We felt she was our responsibility, especially during her dating years. But now that she's married to McKinnon all is well," he added.

"Have they been married long?"

He shook his head. "Since the end of November. Cole and I couldn't ask for a better man for our sister."

Alyssa smiled. "That's a nice thing to say."

"It's the truth. Although we do sympathize with him most of the time. Casey can be pretty damn headstrong so McKinnon has his work cut out for him."

"So your immediate family consists of your brother and your sister?"

"We used to think that. My mother was Uncle Sid's sister and she came to live with him at the ranch when her husband was supposedly killed during a rodeo and she was left carrying triplets."

Alyssa slanted him a confused look. "*Supposedly* was killed?"

"Yes, that's the story she and Uncle Sid fabricated for everyone when in fact our father was very much alive. However, she felt she was doing him a favor by not telling him she was pregnant and disappearing. So Cole, Casey and I grew up believing our father was dead."

"When did you find out differently?"

"On Mom's deathbed. She wanted us to know the truth."

Alyssa immediately recalled her grandfather's deathbed confession. He'd revealed that he was her biological father and not her grandfather. It had been a confession that had changed her life forever, one that had caused jealousy within the family—a family that had never been close anyway. "What happened after that?"

He smiled over at her and she knew what he was thinking. She asked a lot of questions. Gramps would always tell her that, too. Thinking of the man whom for years she'd thought of as her grandfather sent a warm feeling through her.

"After that, Cole and I decided to find our father and develop a relationship with him. We knew it wouldn't be easy, considering we would be a surprise to him and the fact that we were grown men in our late twenties."

That hadn't been too long ago, she mused, considering he was thirty-two now. Probably around the same time she had been learning the truth about her own parentage. "Did you find him?"

He gave another chuckle, this one just as sensitive to her flesh as the other had been. "Yes, we found him, all right. And we found something else right along with him."

"What?"

"A slew of cousins we didn't know we had. Westmorelands from just about everywhere. We suddenly found ourselves part of a big family and it was a family that welcomed us with open arms. They've made us feel as if we were a part of them so quickly it was almost overwhelming."

Alyssa studied the sound of his voice and could tell that even now for him it was still overwhelming. He was blessed to be a part of such a loving and giving group. There, however, was one thing she'd noted. He hadn't mentioned how his sister had taken the revelation of the missing father.

"Your sister, how did she handle meeting her father for the first time?" she asked.

A part of her needed to know. She knew how she had handled it when she'd discovered that Isaac Barkley was her father and not her grandfather. A part of her had wished he would have told her sooner. That would have explained a lot of things and then the two of them would have been able to face the jealousy and hatred together. But he had died, leaving her all alone.

"It was harder for Casey to come around and accept things. She'd believed what Mom had told us all those years. She wasn't ready to meet a father who was very much alive. It took her a while to form a relationship with him, but that's all in the past now. In fact she moved to Montana to be close to him. She met McKinnon there and fell in love."

Alyssa sighed. A part of her wished she could find

someone and fall in love but she knew that wouldn't be possible as long as Kimberly Barkley still existed on this earth. Kimberly was determined to destroy whatever bit of happiness came Alyssa's way.

"This is the entrance to the ranch, Alyssa."

Alyssa leaned forward and glanced out the windshield and side windows and caught her breath. What she saw all around her was spellbinding. Simply breathtaking. She had lived on a small ranch in Houston for the first thirteen years of her life and had loved it. Then one day, her mother had sent her away to live with her grandfather in the city. That was probably the one most decent thing her mother had ever done in her life.

"It's beautiful, Clint. How big is it?" Everywhere she looked she saw ranges, fields and meadows. She couldn't imagine waking up to this view every morning, every single day.

"If you include the reserve on the south ridge it's over fifty thousand acres. Uncle Sid was a ladies' man who never married and so he left the ranch to me, Cole and Casey."

Alyssa nodded. She didn't want to consider the possibility, didn't want to imagine how it would feel for once to not have to worry about Kim dropping in just make her life a living hell. The truck, she noticed, had stopped, and she lifted a brow as she glanced over at Clint.

He smiled. "I want to show you something."

He got out of the truck and she followed and he led her close to a cliff. "Look down there," he said, pointing.

And she did. It was then that she saw his ranch, sitting down in the valley below. It was huge, a monstrosity of a house that was surrounded by several barns and other buildings. There was a corral full of horses and she could barely see the figures of men below who were working with the horses. "It's absolutely stunning, Clint," she said, turning to him. It was then that she became aware of just how close they were standing, of the heat his closeness had generated and how the darkening of his eyes was beginning to stir a caress across her flesh.

She moved to take a step back and his hand reached out to her waist, to assist her, or so it seemed. But his hand stayed there and his touch burned her skin through the thin material of her blouse. Her gaze left his eyes and moved to his lips, the one part of him that had always fascinated her. The fullness of them made her imagine just how they would feel on hers. She thought they would be soft to the touch at first, but they would become demanding and hungry as soon as they connected with hers.

She wasn't a forward person, but one thing Gramps had always taught her was that sometimes, if it was something you really wanted, you just had to take the bull by the horns. Well, she intended to do just that.

He was bending his head toward her, or maybe she imagined that he was doing so. And just to be sure, she leaned forward and slid her hands over his chest. The first touch of his lips on hers sent pleasure points in her body on high alert and when she parted her lips on a sigh, he entered her mouth in one delicious sweep.

He tasted hot. He tasted like a man. And she settled into his kiss as if it was her right to do so. With their mouths locked together, their tongues tangled, stroked and slid everywhere. And then in a move she would have thought was impossible, he thrust his tongue deeper inside her mouth, causing her to instinctively latch on to it, suck it and stroke it some more. This was what you called total mouth concentration, the solicitation of participation and the promise of satisfaction. Everything was there in this kiss. And Clint Westmoreland was delivering in a way that made the quiet existence she had carved out for herself the last two years a waste of good time and energy.

The kiss was incredible, she thought, sinking deeper into it. She might have regrets later but now she needed this. Her entire body felt as if this was what she was supposed to be doing. And considering this was the first day she had seen him in over five years, the very thought of that was crazy and…

Clint abruptly broke off the kiss. He drew much-needed air into his lungs and fought the urgent pull in his loins. *How had he let this happen? Where was that control he was famous for? Where was his will to deny anything he thought might threaten his livelihood?*

He didn't say anything to Alyssa. He just stood there and stared at her while trying to get the rampant beating of his heart under control. Trying to fight the sensations overtaking him. She had been kissing him as passionately as he had been kissing her. At first her lack of kissing experience had surprised him, but she was a quick study. The moment his tongue came into play, she'd allowed hers to do the same, and without any hesitation.

"Okay, Clint, what was all that about?" she asked in a quiet tone.

She was staring at him while licking her lips. The intimate gesture made his stomach clench. "I think," he murmured, "that I should ask you the same thing. That wasn't a kiss taken, Alyssa, but one that was shared."

He waited for her to deny his words but she didn't. Instead she turned away from him and glanced back down to look at his ranch house. And before she could ask he said, "I'll promise to keep my desire under wraps for the next thirty days."

For a moment she didn't say anything, didn't make a move to even acknowledge that he had spoken. And then she looked back at him and at that moment a wave of desire, more intense than anything he'd ever encountered, raced through him.

"Can you?" she asked softly.

Holding her gaze, he was having a hard time keeping up. "Can I what?"

"Bottle your desire for thirty days." He watched as she inhaled deeply, drew herself up as if she was trying to take back control of the situation and he saw her eyes go from sensuous to serious. "I need to know before I make any decision about staying here with you."

He frowned. Was she afraid of him? He covered the distance separating them and came to a stop in front of her. Forcing her to look up at him, become the main focus of her attention. "Let me explain one thing about me, Alyssa," he said in a voice that he knew had her complete attention. "You don't have anything to fear if you stay here, least of all me. You set the boundaries and I will abide by them. I don't have a woman in my life right now, nor do I need one. What you see down there is my life. You are my wife in name only. I will remember that. I will respect that. But after the thirty days I expect you to go, just like I'm sure you'll want to leave. I don't have time for involvements. The only thing long-term in my life is this ranch and the running of it and the foundation. Those things are all I need. They are all I want."

At his blunt words she asked, "Then why did you kiss me?"

Clint saw her eyes were flashing and knew she was beginning to take what he was saying personally. "The reason *we* kissed each other," he said slowly, "is because of a number of things. Curiosity. Need. Desire. It was best that we took care of all three before we got to the ranch. Trust me, you won't become an itch that I'll be tempted to scratch."

Alyssa frowned, not sure she liked the way he'd said that. Had he found her kiss so lacking that he'd not be tempted to do it again? Kim had always said when it came to men she presented no appeal, or that she wouldn't recognize pleasure if it came up to her and bit her. Clint had certainly made a liar out of her cousin. Under his lips she had definitely recognized pleasure. She had actually drowned in it.

"Now," he said, interrupting her thoughts. "Do you want to go down to the ranch with me or would you prefer that I take you back into town?"

She glared at him. "I haven't made up my mind about anything."

"I didn't say you had. I just want you to have peace of mind in doing so."

Behind Clinton's terse words, she suspected he was low on tolerance. But then she'd come to that same conclusion earlier at the diner. She glanced down the valley at the ranch and then she glanced back at Clint. "I'm still staying at the ranch for the night."

"Then let's go. I've got plenty to do when I get there."

When they got back in the truck and he turned the ignition, she glanced out the window when the truck started moving. She had gotten her real taste of passion from the man who was her husband—at least on paper. And she had surrendered without thought or hesitation.

For some reason she sensed a wild streak in Clint, one that he probably didn't even know was there. A wildness she detected, one that had almost come out in their kiss. As far as she was concerned the man had desire bottled and it was fighting to become uncorked. If it ever broke free she didn't want to think of the consequences, the combustion or the fiery, hot passion.

And if that happened, was there a woman in this world who would be able to tame Clint Westmoreland? she wondered.

Four

Inviting Alyssa to spend the night at the ranch wasn't the smartest thing he'd ever done, Clint decided.

From the cliff the ranch house looked huge. But when you stood directly in front of it and got a close-up view, you got a clear picture of just how spacious it was. He hoped Alyssa would decide that in a house as large as his they could easily avoid each other for four short weeks.

The front door opened and Chester walked out. The man, who for years had been Clint's cook, housekeeper, and if there was need, ranch hand, was big. He stood at least six-four and weighed over two hundred and fifty pounds. At sixty-five he looked intimidating and mean as a bear. Once you got to know him, however, it didn't take long to see he was as soft and easygoing as a teddy bear.

Clint knew that Chester considered himself a surrogate father to the triplets. The old man was quick to brag that he'd helped Doc Shaw deliver the three. For that reason—in Clint's opinion—Chester lived under the false assumption that he knew what was best for them. He had been the one to convince Clint and Cole to find the father they hadn't known they had, and the one to talk Casey into building a relationship with their father.

And now with Casey happily married and living in Montana, Chester was on a bandwagon to get Clint and Cole to follow suit. He felt marriage should be in their future plans, the not-so-distant future. Chester claimed he wanted them to find the bliss he'd found in his own happy marriage of over thirty years. His beloved wife Ada died a few years ago. Even now everyone still missed the presence of the gentle and kind woman who had been the love Chester's life.

Clint saw the way Chester was sizing Alyssa up. The old man was trying to see if she appeared sturdy enough to handle the roughness of a working ranch, and if she had enough brawn to handle Clint. According to Chester, the Golden Glade Ranch needed a mistress who was strong in both mind and body. Clint knew Chester believed Clint needed a woman who could take him on with fortitude.

He had told Chester that morning about the agency's mistake. Now he dreaded telling the old man he and Alyssa were being forced to live as man and wife for thirty days. Chester would somehow see such a thing as a sign that somebody up there was trying to tell Clint something. Clint easily recognized the calculating look in Chester's eyes and frowned.

"I know I've said it already, Clint, but your home is beautiful," Alyssa said.

Alyssa's words reclaimed Clint's attention. He moved his gaze from Chester and back to her. The side of her face was highlighted by the sun. The soft glow of her features made him remember their kiss and how good she had tasted. Even now he wouldn't mind devouring her mouth again, relishing her taste once more. She glanced over at him and he felt a fierce tug in his stomach. He didn't like the feeling one damn bit.

Knowing she expected a response from him, he said, "Thanks. Let me introduce you to Chester and then I'll show you around."

As if impatient for an introduction, Chester came down the steps and went directly to Alyssa, offered her his hand and gave a half laugh and said, "Welcome to the Golden Glade. So you're Clint's wife. We're mighty glad to have you." Before she could respond he added, "And you're just what Clint needs around here."

And at that moment, Clint actually felt like slugging him.

The man's words drew Alyssa up short. It was true that she and Clint were legally married, but as far as she was concerned it was nothing more than a mistake on paper. A mistake that needed to be rectified. But a comment like that made her aware of the seriousness of their situation and just how quickly they needed to resolve the matter.

Not sure how to respond to Chester, Alyssa decided not to address his statement of their marital status and to accept his comment on the ranch by saying, "It's a beautiful ranch."

Clint had walked around the truck and appeared at her side. She glanced up at him and saw he was frowning at the older man. Evidently he hadn't appreciated the reminder of their situation, either.

"Thanks, and Clint is doing a fine job keeping it that way," Chester said. "But what I've told him numerous times is that what this ranch needs is a—"

"Alyssa, this is Chester. Cook and housekeeper," Clint said, smoothly interrupting whatever it was the older man had been about to say.

Not to be outdone the man merely nodded. "What this ranch needs is a woman's touch," he said as if he had not been interrupted.

Alyssa's thoughts began to whirl. *Why would Chester make such a comment? Didn't he know that her and Clint's marriage wasn't real?* She gave a quick glance at Clint but his features were unreadable. Deciding it wasn't her place to meddle in what was going on between Clint and one of his employees, she turned her attention back to Chester and said, "It's nice meeting you, Chester."

The man gave her a huge smile. "No, Alyssa, it is nice meeting *you*. Come on in and I'll show you around."

"No, I'll be showing Alyssa around," Clint said.

Both Alyssa and Chester turned to Clint. "I thought you had a lot of work to do," Chester said.

Alyssa had thought the very same thing and watched

as Clint shrugged massive shoulders before he said, “What I have to do can wait.”

Alyssa glanced back at Chester and for a quick second she could have sworn she’d seen a sparkle in the old man’s eyes. “Suit yourself then,” Chester said. “I need to start dinner, anyway.” And then Alyssa watched as the older man gave her a final smile before going back into the house.

“I’ll take you to the guest room you’ll be using before giving you a tour,” Clint said.

Alyssa turned in time to see Clint walk over to the truck to get her overnight bag. She inclined her head as she continued to watch him. The man had such a sensuous walk, she thought.

As if he’d felt her eyes on him, he turned with a concerned look on his face. ”Is everything all right, Alyssa?” he asked quietly.

She suddenly felt the need to hug her arms and protect herself from his intense gaze, but she didn’t. Instead she appreciated his thoughtful consideration. No one had asked if everything was all right with her since her grandfather’s death. “Yes, I’m fine. Thanks for asking,” she said.

He only nodded before opening the truck door to pull out her bag. He then turned and walked back toward her. She knew that he was uncomfortable with the situation they had been placed in and he didn’t like it any more than she did. But, they would work things out. She’d discovered five years ago that Clint Westmoreland was a man who could handle just about anything that came his way. She saw that strength in him and admired him for it.

"Come this way," he said. She noticed he had come to a stop directly in front of her. His closeness caused her to breathe unevenly and she swallowed deeply to get control of her emotions. It wasn't as if they hadn't spent time together before. While working that assignment five years ago, for one full week they'd been almost glued at the hip, trying to make their cover believable. They'd even shared a hotel room—although at night she would take the bed and he would crash on the sofa. But still they had shared close quarters and although she had been fully aware of him as a man, his presence hadn't affected her like it did now.

It seemed she was now more aware of the opposite sex. Actually, in this case, she was more aware of Clint Westmoreland. She had been fascinated with him when they'd worked together, but now he took her breath away. And back then she had been so focused on doing a good job on her first assignment as a Ranger that everything else, including Clint, had been secondary. But that was not the case now. *How on earth would she survive under the same roof with this man for thirty days?*

He opened the door for her and then stood back for her to enter. Her stomach knotted and she felt her senses tingling. She had a feeling that once she walked over the threshold her life would never be the same.

Steeling himself, Clint watched as Alyssa entered his home. He couldn't recall the last time he had been so fully aware of a woman to the point that everything about her—even her scent was registering in his mind—seemed branded onto his brain cells.

If she decided to stay the thirty days, she would only be here for a short while, he reminded himself. He could handle that. His work days at the ranch were long and grueling. If he just kept his mind on the job at hand—running the ranch and keeping his uncle's legacy alive—he would be fine.

His thoughts shifted back to Alyssa as he watched her stand in the middle of his living room glancing around. She seemed in awe, incapable of speaking. Had she thought just because he spent most of his time outdoors that he didn't appreciate having nice things indoors?

"Everything is so beautiful," she said in a low voice when she began to speak.

He wasn't reluctant to agree and said thanks. "I hired an interior decorator to do her thing throughout the house. Especially in the guest rooms."

She glanced over at him. "Do you get a lot of visitors?"

He chuckled. "Yes. The Westmoreland family is a rather large one and they love to visit. They like checking up on each other. I have a bunch of cousins who were close growing up. Like I said earlier, when they found out about me, Cole and Casey, they didn't hesitate in extending that closeness to us."

He glanced at his watch. "Come on and let me show you to your room so you can get settled in. I'll show you the rest of the house later."

* * *

A few moments later Alyssa's fingers trembled as she ran them across the richness of the guest room furniture. There had to be about ten or so guest rooms in this house. Clint had been quick to explain that his uncle loved to entertain and always had friends visiting.

The layout of the house actually suited the magnificent structure. Once you entered the front door you walked into this huge foyer that led into a huge living room. There was also an eat-in kitchen and dining room. The house had four wings that jutted off from the living room. North, south, east and west. Clint's bedroom was huge and was located on the north wing, and although he'd only given her a quick glimpse, she'd liked what she'd seen of it.

The beauty of every room in his home made her speechless. It seemed to be fitting for a king…and his queen, from the expensive furniture to the costly portraits that hung on the walls. He evidently was a man who liked nice things and who didn't mind paying his money for them.

Clint had left her alone to get settled and indicated he would be back in a few minutes. She knew he was trying not to crowd her, give her space and she appreciated that. She wondered at what point her heart would stop beating so wildly in her chest. When would the rapid flutter in her stomach cease?

She glanced over at the overnight bag. It contained her toiletries, fresh underwear, an extra-large T-shirt to sleep in and a pair or jeans and a top. If she decided to stay the thirty days she would have to return to Waco and pack more of her things. She supposed that her friends were wondering where she had gone. She hadn't mentioned her destination or the reason for her trip to anyone except her aunt Claudine. Aunt Claudine wouldn't tell anyone about her trip, Alyssa thought with a chuckle. Her sixty-year-old great-aunt would be tickled that for once she knew something that the other family members didn't.

Alyssa had already put away the few things she'd brought with her and was waiting for Clint when he knocked on the bedroom door. For some reason she felt restless and a call to Aunt Claudine hadn't helped when she was informed that Kim had already begun asking questions about her whereabouts.

When Clinton knocked again she quickly crossed the room, not wanting him to think she had taken a nap or something. She opened the door. He stood in the hallway, towering over her. "I told you that I'd be back. Are you ready for me to show you around?"

Looking up at him, his penetrating dark gaze seemed to hold her captive and she became aware of how even more fluttering was going on in her stomach. And it wasn't helping matters that she felt compelled to stare at his lips. Doing so reminded her of the kiss they had shared and how the moment his tongue had wrapped around hers an ache had begun within her. It was an ache that wouldn't go away.

At that moment she wasn't sure if going anywhere with him was a smart move. That and the fact that she seemed to be glued to the spot. But then she quickly decided that she wasn't about to let another man get to her again. Kevin had taught her a lesson she would never forget. She studied Clint's features again. They were still unreadable. "Clint…"

"Yes?"

He took a step closer, stepping into the room, and since she was glued to the spot she couldn't get her legs to move. She inclined her head back and looked up at him, thinking he was so tall, and much too handsome. She then saw the dark frown that creased his forehead. "What's wrong?" she asked. The words had come tumbling out before she could hold them in.

One of his broad shoulders lifted nonchalantly. "You tell me," he said.

She had said his name; however, because of the way he had been looking at her, the way that look had made blood rush through her veins, she had forgotten what she'd been about to say. She then remembered. "I was going to say that if you're busy I can just look around myself."

"I'm not busy, so let's go," he said.

She noticed right before he turned to step back into the hallway that the frown on his face had deepened, and she had a feeling that although he had invited her to stay for the night he still didn't like it one bit that she was there.

After giving Alyssa a tour of his home, he walked by her side down the steps to the outside. Her compliments had again pleased him, although he wasn't quite sure why they had. He'd never been one to place a lot of emphasis on what anyone thought of what he owned. He bought to satisfy his taste and not anyone else's.

"You said your sister moved to Montana. Does she come back to visit often?"

He glanced over at Alyssa as they walked down the stairs. She seemed to have gotten shorter and a quick look at her feet told him why. She had exchanged her three-inch high-heel shoes for a pair of flats. Smart move. A working ranch was no place for high heels. "Casey's been back once since she left and that was to get her wedding dress made. Mrs. Miller, a seamstress in town, always said she wanted to be the one who designed Casey's wedding dress if she ever got married," he said.

Her question quickly reminded him of something. "But she and McKinnon might be visiting within the next couple of weeks. Why?"

She shrugged her shoulders. "I was just wondering." And then she asked, "What about Cole?"

He glanced over at her again. "What about him?"

"Does he live here, too?"

"No, Cole has a place in town but most of the time he's on assignment somewhere." Clint had an idea why Alyssa asked about Casey and Cole and the chances that they would being paying a visit to the ranch anytime soon. "If you're concerned what my siblings will have to say about our situation if they happen to pop in then don't be. They won't ask questions."

At the uncertainty in her eyes, he went on to say, "And no, it's not because I usually let women stay over on occasion. It's just that my family respects my privacy. Besides, it's not like either of us has done anything wrong."

"So you plan to tell them the truth about who I am?"

"The part about you being my wife?"

"Yes."

He met her gaze. "I see no reason not to. Besides, Chester knows and if he knows then they know, or they will soon. He thinks I need a wife."

"Why does he think that?"

"He's afraid that like Uncle Sid, I'll get so involved with my horses that I won't take time out to build a personal life or have a family. He's determined not to let that happen. He would marry me off in a heartbeat if he could."

They said nothing for the next few moments, but as they continued to walk together around the ranch he was fully aware of the admiring glances Alyssa was getting from the men who worked for him. His mouth thinned; for some reason he was bothered by it.

"This is a huge place," she said, as if wanting to change the subject, which was okay with him.

"Yes, it is."

"Do you have a lot of men working for you?"

"Well over a hundred. And as I said earlier, Alyssa, if you decide to stay here, the chances of getting in each other's way are slim to none." As far as he was concerned life would be much easier, less complicated that way. The last thing he needed was for her or any woman to get under his skin.

"Ready to head back?" he asked and watched how she pushed a wayward curl back away from her face.

"Yes…and thanks for the tour."

As they walked back toward the ranch house—strolling quietly side by side—he wished like hell he could dismiss from his mind the memory of her taste that remained on his tongue, and how even now, the memory of his lips locked to hers was uncoiling sensations that were running rampant throughout his body. His loins were on fire just thinking about it. His body, in its own way, was sending a reminder of just how long it had been since he'd slept with a woman. It had been way too long and today he was feeling it right down to the bone.

That wasn't good. He had told her that she wouldn't become an itch that he couldn't scratch and he hoped like hell that he didn't live to regret those words. He had to remain calm, in control and more than anything he had to remember that no matter how much desire was eating away at his senses, the last thing he needed in his life was a wife.

Five

"I tell you, Alyssa, that girl is up to no good."

Alyssa tugged off her earring and switched her cell phone to the other ear. Claudine often said that about Kim, but in this case she was inclined to believe her great-aunt. She hadn't heard from Kim in months, at least not since her cousin's last attempt to sabotage one of the projects she'd been working on for a client.

It had cost Alyssa two weeks of production time and she had had to work every hour nonstop to meet the deadline date she'd been given. Of course, as usual, Kim had denied everything and there hadn't been any way Alyssa could prove her guilt.

"You're probably right, Aunt Claudine, but there's nothing that I can do. You know Kim, she's full of surprises." Usually those surprises cost Alyssa tremendously. Kim's bag of dirty tricks included everything from sabotaging important projects to sleeping with Alyssa's fiancé and then having a courier deliver the damaging photographs just moments before she was to leave her home for the church.

Her troubles with Kim started when Alyssa had arrived in the Barkleys' household to live with her grandfather and great-aunt. Her mother had never given Alyssa a reason for sending her away, but to this day Alyssa believed that Kate Harris had begun to notice her most recent lover's interest in her thirteen-year-old-daughter's developing body.

As Alyssa was growing up, her mother had never told her the identity of her father. In fact, Alyssa was very surprised to learn that she had a paternal grandfather. Right before her mother had put her on the plane for Waco, she had told Alyssa that she was the illegitimate daughter of Isaac Barkley's dead son, Todd. Todd had been killed in the line of duty as a Texas Ranger.

Alyssa had arrived in Waco feeling deserted and alone, but it didn't take long to see that the arrival of Grandpa Isaac and Aunt Claudine in her life was a blessing of the richest kind. They immediately made her feel wanted, loved and protected.

Unfortunately, her new relatives' acts of kindness didn't sit too well with her cousin Kim, who was the same age as Alyssa. Kim was the daughter of Grandpa Isaac's only other son, Jessie. Jessie's wife had died when Kim was six. From what Alyssa had been told,

Jessie had felt guilty about driving his wife to commit suicide because of his unfaithful ways and had spoiled Kim rotten to ease his guilt. Kim was used to getting all the attention and hadn't liked it one bit when that attention shifted with Alyssa's arrival.

Alyssa couldn't remember a single time Kim had not been a thorn in her side. First, there had been all those devious pranks Kim had played so that Alyssa could get blamed. Fortunately, Grandpa Isaac had known what Kim was doing and had come to her defense. But instead of things getting better, the more Grandpa Isaac stood up for her, the worse Kim got.

Alyssa's teen years had been the hardest and if it hadn't been for her grandfather and great-aunt she doubted she would have gotten through them. And it didn't help matters that her mother never came to visit her, never bothered contacting her at all. Kim liked to claim that Alyssa was living off the Barkleys' charity and that there were some in the family who didn't believe that Todd Barkley had been her father anyway. That claim hadn't bothered Alyssa, because she could see that she favored her grandfather too much not to be his grandchild. Before he'd died everyone had found out that she had actually been his child. It had been a revelation that had shocked the entire family, especially when he had left her an equal share of everything. And in Kim's eyes, Alyssa's inheritance had been the ultimate betrayal.

"Alyssa..."

Her aunt pulled her thoughts back to the present. "Yes, Aunt Claudine?"

"Will staying with that man for a month be so bad? At least the marriage will be dissolved…if that's what you really want."

A smile touched Alyssa's lips. Her aunt was trying to play matchmaker again. "Of course that's what I want. It's what Clint and I both want. We don't know each other and like he said, we are victims of someone's mistake. I really don't think it's fair that we have to suffer because of it," Alyssa explained.

She heard her aunt chuckling. "I can't imagine having to suffer if I was to live under the same roof with a gorgeous man…and you did say he was gorgeous, didn't you?"

Yes, she had said that, and had meant it, as well. Clint's physical features were something she could not lie about. And that in itself was the kicker. Kevin had been a good-looking man but he couldn't hold a candle to Clint. She had never been this aware of a man in her life. "Yes, Auntie, he is a hunk."

"Then I suggest that you stay right there in Austin since your only other option is to bring him here to live. Can you imagine all the commotion that would cause? And it would give Kim another excuse to sharpen her claws and do some damage."

Alyssa had thought of that. She wanted to believe that Clint would not be the weakling that Kevin had been and that he would be able to resist Kim's charms. But usually all it took was for any man to set eyes on Kim and they were done for. Men would actually pause when she walked into a room. Too bad beauty was only skin deep, Alyssa thought.

"I'll ship you some things, Alyssa. Besides, a month away from this circus of a family will do you some good," Claudine said.

Funny, she had thought the same thing. "I have to think things through tonight and give Clint my decision in the morning. If I decide to stay I'll let you know."

"All right, I won't say anything to the others. Eleanor's daughter swears she saw Kim and Kevin together at some nightclub. Can you imagine the two of them seeing each other again after all they did to you? We heard Kevin got a promotion with that company he works for. That's probably why Kim is back in the picture. She's determined to land a rich husband one way or the other."

In a perverse way Alyssa wished her cousin the best. Even with all the low-down and underhanded things that Kim had done, Alyssa couldn't find it in her heart to hate her. She had tried when she'd gotten those photos of Kim and Kevin in bed together, but now all she could do was feel pity for them both. The thought that he and Kim were seeing each other no longer bothered her. Any love she might have had for him ended the day that should have been her wedding day. If Kim was the type of woman he preferred then more power to him.

She wondered just what type of woman Clint would prefer. She could see a beautiful woman in his arms, in his bed, giving birth to his babies. Alyssa was certain she didn't fit the criteria for Clint's dream woman. She was of average design and she didn't fit the "dream-woman" mold. The only reason they were married now was because of someone's screwup. Even when they'd worked together he hadn't given her a second thought, although they had shared a hotel room for a week. Alyssa could not forget sharing such close quarters with him, inhaling his scent, breathing the same air, or sitting across a table and sharing food with Clint Westmoreland.

That made her think of the meal they had shared less than an hour ago. Chester had prepared a delicious meal, but it had been just the two of them. She couldn't help but notice that the older man, although still extremely friendly, hadn't been as chatty as he'd been when she had first arrived. Clint must have said something to him, probably warning him not to put foolish ideas into her head. Not that he could have. She was a realist, almost too much so at times—at least that's what Aunt Claudine claimed. Alyssa would be the first to admit that her dreams of forever after had gotten destroyed the moment she had seen those pictures on her wedding day. It would be hard, nearly impossible for anyone to make a believer out of her again.

She heard a noise outside her bedroom window and crossed the room to see what had caused it. The sun had set and dusk had settled in. One of the floodlights that were shining from the side of the house provided enough brightness for her to see Clint as he leaned against a post talking with two of his men.

It was hard not to take an assessment of Clint each and every time she saw him. From the window, she couldn't see every single detail, but she had a clear view of his thighs. He was standing with his legs braced apart and the muscles that filled his jeans were taut and firm. Just looking at him standing there in that sexy pose made her pulse race. She was actually feeling breathless. *This was her reaction to the man whom she was supposed to live with for thirty days?* She doubted she would be able to get through one day living with him let alone thirty. She was well aware from what he'd said earlier that day about his ability to control his desire if they decided to live together. He had basically given his word that he would abide by any boundaries that she set.

While she was thinking about what boundaries she would establish if she decided to stay, he turned toward the window as if somehow he'd felt her presence there. Their gazes locked. Held. And it seemed at that moment something, a tangible connection she could not define, passed between them. It was as if some understanding had been made, but for the life of her she didn't know what it was.

Dazed and more than a little confused, she took a step back on wobbly knees at the same time she dropped the curtain back in place to shield her from his view. She knew she had to rein in her uncontrollable imagination, urges and lust. If he could control his then she most certainly should be able to get a handle on hers. But she had to admit what she was experiencing was not something she encountered every day. She simply had never been the type of woman to get goggle-eyed over a man. But ever since she'd arrived in Austin, she had been doing that very thing.

Sighing deeply, she moved toward the bathroom hoping her new state of mind was something she got over real soon.

Clint frowned as he walked down the long hallway toward his bedroom. It was way past midnight. After taking care of the evening chores, he had hung around the bunkhouse and played a game of cards with some of his men.

He had stayed away from the house as long as he could, and now he was back inside. His mind wandered to what had happened earlier. He'd been standing out in the yard talking to a couple of his men until he happened to notice Alyssa staring at him from her bedroom window. He'd done the only thing he could do at the time, which was to stare back.

It seemed that against his will, his gaze had locked on hers. It was plain to see that Alyssa was getting to him and the brazen images of her that had been forming in his mind all day weren't helping. Hell, he may have bitten off more than he could chew in asking her to stay under his roof. If only there had been another way for them to end their marriage, he mused. Surely there was someone he could talk to about it.

His cousin Jared immediately came to mind. Jared was the attorney in the family. His specialty was the handling of divorce cases. Perhaps his cousin could give him some advice. He checked his watch. Jared was usually up late at night and Clint turned in the direction of his office, deciding to give his cousin a call.

He pushed open his office door and paused. There, sitting at his desk in front of his computer, was Alyssa. She hadn't heard him enter, and so he just stood for a moment and gazed at her. The soft lighting from the lamp, as well as the glow from the computer screen, seemed to beam on her, highlighting her features. Her hair was no longer hanging around her shoulders. She had pulled it up into a knot at the back of her neck.

Her full attention was on the computer screen and he watched her as she sat in front of it. Her head was tilted in such a way that showed off the slimness of her neck and her shoulders. She sat with perfect posture.

She seemed to be wearing an oversize T-shirt. On anyone else there probably would not have been a single provocative thing about her attire, but on Alyssa, just the part he saw was totally alluring. The way she was sitting made the shirt stretch tight across her chest, and he could plainly see the tips of her nipples. She wasn't wearing a bra. His fingers seemed to twitch and he knew he would love the feel of his fingers slowly stroking the budded tips.

His gaze moved to her face at the same time she parted her lips in a smile before she released a satisfied chuckle. Clint shifted his gaze from her lips to the computer screen to see what held her concentration. She was playing one of those games you downloaded off the Internet. *Alyssa.* She was busy trying to accomplish some goal and from the look of things, she was succeeding.

Deciding it was time to let her know that he was

there, he stepped into the room. "Umm, that looks interesting. Can I play?"

She whirled in her seat and startled dark eyes seemed to clash with his as she stood abruptly. "I'm sorry. I should have asked to use your computer before—"

"You didn't have to ask, Alyssa," he said, interrupting her apology. "You are more than welcome to use it. Please sit back down and continue what you were doing. You seem to be having fun. What is it?"

She hesitated briefly before retaking her seat. Slowly her gaze slid from him to the computer screen. The one thing he had noticed when she stood was that the T-shirt was even more sensually appealing than he'd first thought. It barely covered her thighs and if that wasn't bad enough, it outlined her curves in a way that had blood racing through his veins.

"It's a game called Playing with Fire," she said softly and he had a feeling he was making her nervous. She glanced back over at him. "Have you ever played Atomic Bomberman before?"

He smiled, inwardly fighting the acute desire he felt at that moment. "No, I don't believe that I have," he said.

"Oh. Playing with Fire is sort of a flashy remake of Atomic Bomberman. The object of the game is to blow up your opponent before they blow you up," she explained.

Clint chuckled. "That sounds rather interesting. I take it you like playing games on the computer."

She shrugged. "Yes, it's a way for me to unwind. Whenever I can't sleep I usually get up and play a game or two," she said.

He leaned against the closed door. "I see. Is there a reason you can't sleep?" Already his mind was thinking of his own version of Playing with Fire and the various ways it could be played. "Is the bed not comfortable?" Although he wished it wouldn't go there, his mind quickly thought of her in that huge bed alone.

"No, the bed is fine, really comfortable," she responded with what he denoted as a soft chuckle before adding, "It's just that I'm not used to sleeping in any bed but my own."

"I see."

She cleared her throat before standing again. "Well, I don't want to keep you out of your office," she uttered as she prepared to leave.

"You're not. I had come in to use the phone, but I can make the call from my bedroom just as easily. I'll leave you to your game." He paused a second then asked, "By the way, who's winning?"

He saw the smile that touched her lips, the sparkle that lit her eyes and the proud lifting of her chin. "I am, of course," she answered.

"Now why doesn't that surprise me? Good night, Alyssa," he said, returning her smile.

"Good night, Clint."

Clint turned and moved toward the door. When he felt the sudden rush of blood to his loins he muttered a curse under his breath and turned back around. Before Alyssa could blink he crossed the room and pulled her from the chair. The moment her body was pressed against his and her lips parted in a startled gasp, his mouth swept down on hers at an angle that called for deep penetration. He took hold of her tongue, wanting the taste of her again with a need that was hitting him all at once, and when she returned the kiss—their tongues participated in one hell of a heated duel—a disturbing acceptance entered his mind. He was not prone to giving in to sexual desires like this, he thought. He could get turned on just like the next guy, but never to this magnitude. His response to any woman had never been this strong, this intense, this mind-bogglingly obsessive. The more he tasted her, the more he wanted, and it wasn't helping matters that she felt perfectly right in his arms. Her softness felt so good against his hardness. *What the hell was wrong with him?*

He quickly decided he would have to figure out this change in him later, but not right now. Not when she'd wrapped her arms around his neck and pressed her body closer to his, and not when he could feel the tips of her breasts through the cotton of his shirt. His mind began imagining all sorts of things. He imagined how it would feel to have the tips of those breasts in his mouth, to toy with them using his tongue, or how he would love to spread her on his desk and take her there. Then there was the idea of him sitting in the chair and tugging her down in his lap and…

She suddenly broke the kiss and he watched as she backed away while forcing air into her lungs. He was doing likewise. He was breathing like he had just run a marathon, but each time he inhaled, her scent filled his nostrils. It was a scent that was getting him aroused all over again.

She lifted her head to look at him and that's when he noticed the knot in her hair had come undone and it was flowing wildly around her shoulders, making her look even sexier than before.

"Was that supposed to be a good-night kiss?" Her voice was soft and breathy.

That hadn't been what he'd expected her to say. Actually, he had expected her to dress him down in the worse possible way. *Was it possible that she was admitting that she had wanted the kiss as much as he had?* She didn't seem to be placing the blame entirely on him, although he had been the one to make the first move.

He leaned back against the door as his gaze went to her mouth. "Yes, it was a good-night kiss," he said. "Want another one?"

"No. I doubt if I could handle it," she responded, shaking her head.

A smile touched his lips. Again her comment had surprised him. "Sure you can. Do you want me to prove it to you?"

"No, thank you."

He chuckled softly. "In that case, I'll let you get back to your game." Without giving her a chance to say anything else, he opened the door and quickly walked out of the room, closing the door behind him.

He paused for a second thinking it was obvious that they had the hots for each other. If she remained under his roof there was no way he would be able to keep his hands off her. He wondered if the kisses they'd shared would be a determining factor in whether she stayed or went back to Waco. Would living together be too much of a temptation? Thirty days was a long time.

She'd said she wasn't used to sleeping in any bed other than her own. In a way he had been glad to hear that. On the other hand, he figured she had to know that if she remained at the Golden Glade, at the rate they were going, she would eventually share his.

As he made his way toward his bedroom, thinking about the explosive chemistry between them began to annoy the hell out of him. He was a man known to have a multitude of control. In the past when lust consumed his body he had a way of dealing with it. Any available and willing woman would do. But he had a feeling that his usual solution would not work this time. His body wanted only one woman and that wasn't good.

Alyssa released a deep breath the moment Clint closed the door behind him. It was simply amazing that one man could have that kind of effect on her. Every single time she saw him, every time he kissed her the result was the same—passion. *When would the attraction she had for him wear off? What if it never did?*

Maybe she needed to rethink her decision to remain at Clint's ranch for the thirty days. It was a decision she hadn't yet told him she'd made, only because she had mentioned that she would need to sleep on it. And she had, which was the main reason she was up now. Once the decision had been made she couldn't get her body to go back to sleep. It had become restless and for the first time ever, fiercely aroused.

And for him to find her in his office wearing only a large T-shirt was embarrassing. But the house had been quiet for a long while and she figured everyone had gone to bed for the night. His bedroom was in a different wing and so she had assumed the coast was clear. She thought that she could sneak into his office for a while and not be noticed. But he had noticed. And so she made a new promise—no more late-night game-playing on the computer for her.

She inhaled deeply. In the morning she would tell him of her decision to stay. She would also tell him that her decision came with stipulations. He'd said earlier that day, after their first kiss, that he was able to control his desire for her. If kissing her the way he did was his desire under control, she didn't want to think how the kiss would be with those same desires unleashed.

Six

Alyssa's heart immediately began beating harder when she walked into the kitchen the next morning to find Clint seated at the table. Although it appeared he was just starting in on breakfast, she knew he was there waiting on her. His expression indicated that he wanted to know her decision.

She glanced around the large kitchen, trying to ignore the pulse that was erratically thumping in her throat. It was a sin and shame that Clint looked so good this early in the morning. He was staring at her with those dark, piercing eyes of his, and the way the sunlight captured the well-defined planes of his face made him appear hauntingly handsome. Alyssa found his good looks quite disturbing, given the fact she was trying to resist her attraction to him.

Seeing him only reminded her of her behavior with him last night in his office. He had once again kissed her mindless, engulfing her with a degree of passion she thought was possible only in those romance novels Aunt Claudine read. Alyssa had gone to bed dreaming about him, their kiss and the things she wanted to do with him beyond a kiss. She had awakened mortified that such thoughts had entered her mind. She would need to take steps to make sure her dreams never became a reality.

For her own sake and well-being, she had reached the conclusion that setting ground rules with Clint would be the only way they would survive living under the same roof. Otherwise, she was setting herself up for many tiring days and disturbing nights, Alyssa realized.

"Where's Chester?" she asked.

Clint leaned back in his chair. "He's off on Wednesdays. At least, he takes off after breakfast and then returns at dinnertime. It's the day he's at the children's hospital being Snuggles the Clown."

Alyssa lifted a brow. "Snuggles the Clown?"

"He spends his day in the children's ward making the kids laugh. He's been doing it for over twenty years now and he's a big hit. That's how he and Uncle Sid met. Chester used to be a rodeo clown," Clint said.

At first Alyssa couldn't picture Chester as a clown, but then as she thought about it, she changed her mind. He had a friendly air about him and would probably be someone who loved kids. She didn't know any clowns and found the thought of him being one fascinating. "You have to love kids to do something like that," she said.

"He does. It was unfortunate that he and Ada never had any of their own."

"Was Ada his wife?"

"Yes. They were married over thirty years. She died six years ago from an acute case of pneumonia," Clint explained.

"That's sad," she said quietly.

"It was. He took her death pretty hard. They had a very strong marriage."

A very strong marriage. Alyssa wondered if that meant the same thing as the two of them were deeply in love. "So he's been working at the ranch a long time?"

"Yes, Chester's been working here since before I was born," Clint said.

Alyssa could hear something in Clint's voice that went beyond mere likeness of Chester. It was easy to tell that Clint considered Chester more than just a housekeeper and a cook. He considered the man an intricate part of his family. While giving her a tour of the outside of the house, he had introduced her to several of the men who worked for him. Some of them were older and full of experience in the taming of the horses. The younger ones were learning the ropes, but everyone, as Clint had been quick to point out, played an important part in the running of his operation. The men had been friendly and respectful and when he had introduced her as nothing more than a good friend, it was apparent they had accepted his word.

"You'd better dig in while the food is warm," Clint said.

Taking his statement to mean he was tired of answering her questions, she walked over to the stove to fix her plate and pour a cup of coffee, feeling Clint's gaze on her with every move she made.

"I'm glad you know to do that," he said.

She turned and looked at him, bewildered. "Do what?"

"Fix your own food."

At her confused look he said, "A lot of women wouldn't. They would expect to be waited on hand and foot."

Alyssa turned back around to scoop eggs onto her plate wondering if he'd ever met Kim. Her cousin would definitely be one of those type of women. Uncle Jessie still called Kim his princess and she took it literally. "Well, I'm not one of them," she said when she came to the table to sit down. "I'm used to fending for myself."

She had barely taken her seat when Clinton folded his arms across his chest and asked, "Okay, what have you decided?"

Instead of answering him, she stared down into the dark liquid of her coffee for a moment before glancing up at him. "Do you have to know this minute?"

"Any reason you can't tell me this minute?" he countered, with a little irritation in his voice.

She set her cup down knowing the last thing they needed was to get agitated with each other. Besides, he was right. There wasn't a reason she couldn't tell him now. "No, I guess not."

She didn't say anything for a few moments and then

met his gaze. "Before I commit to anything, I want you to agree to something," she said.

He lifted a dark brow. "Agree to what?"

"Agree that you won't try to get me into your bed."

He smiled. "My bed?"

"Or any bed in this house." She thought it best to clarify. "And to be more specific, I want your word that you won't try to seduce me into bed with you."

He laughed softly and held her gaze for a long moment. "Define *seduce,*" he said.

Alyssa was aware that he was toying with her, but she was more determined than ever to make sure he understood her position. "You're a man, Clint. You know very well what seduction entails," she said.

His smile deepened. "And you think I'd do something like that?"

She didn't hesitate in answering. "Yes. I'm certain of it. In less than twenty-four hours we've kissed twice, which leads me to believe you would try seducing me."

He stared at her for a moment, eyed her reflectively and then said, "You're right. I would in a heartbeat." And then he asked, "And we've kissed twice, you say?"

Like he didn't know it. "Yes," she said, now very annoyed.

"Want to go for three?" he murmured in a voice that was so husky that it sent shivers through her body.

She eyed him sternly. "I'm serious, Clint."

"So am I."

She stared into his deep, penetrating gaze. Yes, he

was serious. He was dead serious. The very thought that he wanted to kiss her again, tangle his tongue with hers and taste her, made the breath she was breathing get caught in her throat. *Had he just admitted that he enjoyed kissing her?* Well, she could admit that she enjoyed kissing him, as well. There was something devastatingly mind-blowing about the feel of him thrusting his tongue deep into her mouth, moving it around, latching on to hers and…

"Anything else you want from me?"

She shot him a cool look. "Maybe I'd better add kissing to the mix. I think it's a good idea if we refrain from doing it," she said.

"That can't happen," he said. She noticed that his lips curved into an easy smile.

His response had been quick and decisive. Alyssa tried remaining calm. She felt a rush of blood that gushed through her veins. "Why can't it happen?"

"Because we enjoy kissing too much. The best thing to do is to stay in control when we do kiss. Personally, I don't see anything wrong with us kissing. It's merely a friendly form of greeting," he said.

Yeah. Right. It was a form of greeting that she could do without. Especially because kissing Clint Westmoreland made her want to indulge in other things. Things that were better left alone.

"Like I said, Alyssa," he said, interrupting her thoughts. "The key is self-control. As much as I want you and as much as kissing you places temptation in my path, I promise I won't take our attraction to the next level. I have too much work to do around here to get involved with a woman—in any way," he said.

She admired his iron-clad control…if he really had it. He sounded so confident, so sure of himself, she would love to test his endurance level to see what it could or could not withstand.

"But I have to admit you bring something to the table a lot of women haven't," he said.

She glanced over at him and her pulse jumped at the way he was looking at her.

"And what might that be?" she asked softly.

"Although it's only on paper, you're my wife. Perhaps it is because I've seen things from a male perspective, but it's as if knowing you're bound to me is opening up desires and urges that I usually don't have. The fact that we are married makes me crave things."

She frowned. *In other words, having a woman under his roof was making him horny,* Alyssa quickly surmised. "Then I need to add another condition to my visit. That from a female perspective, whatever desires are opening up for you, I suggest that you take your time and close them. I may not have all the self-control you claim to have, but I have no interest in getting involved with a man—in any way. Besides, if I were to get involved with a man it would have to be serious. I'm not into casual relationships where the only goal is relieving sexual frustrations," she said.

He was silent for a moment as he stared at her, and for a fraction of a second she thought she saw a challenging glint in his gaze. And then he said, "I won't try getting you into my bed…or yours…but I won't promise to keep my mouth to myself. I can't see us denying ourselves that one bit of indulgence."

"Why? When it won't lead anywhere?"

He inclined his head. His gaze locked with hers. "I desire you. Kissing you is a way to work you out of my system. I believe the same could be said for you, as well. At the end of the thirty days I suspect you will be ready to leave as much as I'll be ready for you to leave," he said.

Alyssa held his gaze and read what she saw in his eyes. He really believed that and she would go even further to say he was counting on it.

"Because we would have kissed each other out of our systems by then?" she asked, needing to be sure she understood his logic in all of this.

"Yes," he replied evenly.

"And you think you're that elusive and wild at heart."

He lifted a brow. "Wild at heart?"

"Yes. You don't think there's a woman who exists who's capable of capturing your heart," she said.

"I know there's not."

He had said the words with such venom that she was forced to ask. "Have you ever been in love, Clint?"

She could tell by the look that appeared in his eyes that her question surprised him. She saw the way his shoulders tightened, the firm grip he held on his coffee cup and knew she had waded in turbulent waters.

For a while she thought he wasn't going to respond, but then he did.

"No," he said.

For some reason she didn't believe him. Not that she thought he was lying to her, but she figured that the love he might have had for someone had been so effectively destroyed that it was hard to recall when that emotion had ever gripped his heart. It had been that way for her after she'd discovered what Kevin had done. It was as if her love had gotten obliterated with that one single act of unfaithfulness. She couldn't help wondering about the woman who had crushed Clint's heart.

"Are you satisfied with our agreement?"

Alyssa dragged in a deep breath. The issue of them kissing hadn't been fully resolved to her liking, but the way she saw it, he was not a man to force himself on anyone. If she resisted his kisses enough times, he would find some other game to amuse himself. "Yes, I'm satisfied," she said.

"So, are you agreeing to remain here for thirty days, live under the same roof with me?"

Intimate images flooded her mind. She forced them out. His home was humongous. His bedroom was on one side of the house and hers on the other. Chances were there would be days when their paths wouldn't even cross. "Yes, I'm agreeing to do just that," she said.

He nodded. "I'll call Hightower and let him know. By the way, what about more clothes for you? You only brought an overnight bag," Clint said.

"I spoke with my aunt yesterday and she told me if I decided to stay she would send me some things."

"Your aunt is the only family you have?"

She might as well be, she wanted to say.

"No, I have an uncle and several cousins," she said instead. "My mother sent me to live with my grandfather and Aunt Claudine when I was thirteen. Over the years Aunt Claudine has become a surrogate mother to me," she added.

"And your grandfather?"

A pain settled in her heart. She wanted to correct him so badly.

"My grandfather died four years ago," she said softly.

"That was about the same time I lost my mother," he said, looking down at the coffee in his cup. She could hear the sadness in his voice. He glanced up and at that moment an emotion passed between them—a deep understanding of how it felt to lose someone you truly cared about.

"Were you close to her?" she asked.

"Yes. Casey, Cole and I were her world and she was ours. She and Uncle Sid, along with Chester and the other old-timers on the ranch were our family. What about your mother? You said she sent you to live with your grandfather and aunt when you were thirteen. Do the two of you still keep in touch?"

In a way Alyssa wished he would have asked her anything but that. That her mother could so easily send her away and not stay in touch was still a pain that would occasionally slither through her heart.

"No. I haven't seen or heard from my mother since the day she sent me away," she said.

Deciding she didn't want to subject herself to any more of his inquiries about her family, she stood. "I need to make a few calls. In addition to contacting my aunt, I need to make sure I have everything I need to continue my business while I'm here. That means I will need to use your computer a lot," she said.

"I don't have a problem with that."

Alyssa nodded. "Okay. I'm sure you have a lot to do today, as well," she said, picking up her plate and cup and carrying both over to the sink. "And since today is Chester's day off, I'll take care of the dishes as soon as I've made those calls."

With nothing else to say, Alyssa walked out of the kitchen.

Clint continued to sit at the table. From the moment he had gotten the letter from the bureau advising him of his marriage to Alyssa, he had simply assumed that getting out of the marriage would be easy—a piece of cake. He had miscalculated on a number of things. First, the bureau being so hard-nosed over such a blatant mistake and second, his attraction to the woman who was legally his wife. Now, he was fully committed to go to extraordinary restrictions to keep his hands off of her. In other words, to stay out of her bed and to make sure she stayed out of his.

Neither would be easy.

That was what made the thought of the next thirty days so disconcerting. A part of him wanted to rebel. *Why not have sex with her?* After all it was just sex, no big deal. They were mature adults who evidently had healthy appetites with no desire to get caught up in anything other than the moment. Right? Wrong.

He couldn't help but recall her words about not being one to indulge in casual affairs, which gave him a glimpse into her character. While engaging her in conversation, he had taken in everything she'd said—even some things she hadn't said, especially about her family.

The Texas Ranger in him could detect when someone was withholding information. He hadn't wanted to pry, but she'd deliberately omitted mentioning a few things. Such as why her mother had given her up at thirteen and had never once come back to see her. And when she had mentioned her cousins he hadn't heard that deep sense of love and warmth he'd felt whenever he spoke of his. Granted, he didn't expect every family to be like the Westmorelands, but still he would think there was a closeness there. He had heard the deep love and affection in her voice when she had spoken of her grandfather and aunt.

And then he could very well be reading more into it than was there. It could be that she was a private person and hadn't felt the need or wasn't stirred by any desire to tell him any more than she had. Wife or no wife, it wasn't "expose your soul to Clint" day.

He rubbed his hand down his face. Why did he even care? he wondered. What was there about Alyssa that made him want to dig deeper and unravel her inner being, layer by layer? With that thought in mind, he was about to get up from the table when his cell phone went off. He stood to pull it off the attachment on his belt. "Hello," he said.

"So what's this I hear about you having a wife?"

He couldn't help but smile when he sat back down. He could envision his sister with her long black lashes lifting in a way that said she had every right to know everything she asked him.

"I see Chester's loose lips have been flapping again," he muttered, thinking he needed to have a talk with the old man. Of course, Clint knew that all the talk in the world wouldn't do any good with Chester.

"He knew I had a right to know," Casey Westmoreland Quinn said in a serious tone. "So tell me about her."

He sighed. Since she hadn't asked what happened to make him have a wife in the first place, he could only assume that Chester had covered that information with her already. "What do you want to know?"

"Everything. What's her name? Where is she from? How old is she? Is she someone that you used to work with who I've met already? And so on and so forth."

Clint frowned. Alyssa reminded him of Casey with her endless questions.

"Her name is Alyssa Barkley. She's from Waco and she's twenty-seven. And no, you've never met her. She became a Ranger right out of college and then left not long after that assignment we did together. She was only with the Rangers for a year," he said.

"So you didn't make a good impression on her then, did you?"

"I wasn't trying to. I was all into Chantelle at the time," he said.

"Please don't mention her name," Casey said in feigned terror.

Clint chuckled. Casey and Chantelle had never gotten along from day one. His sister had warned him about her but he wouldn't listen. Now he wished he had. But at the time he had been thinking with the lower part of his body and not his brain. Chantelle caught the attention of any man within one hundred feet. But then so did Alyssa. However, it had taken only a few moments spent with Alyssa to know she and Chantelle were very different.

Alyssa wasn't all into herself. She didn't think she was responsible for the sun rising and setting each day. Chantelle had thought she was all that, and like a testosterone-packed fool, he had played right into her hands without considering the consequences.

"So what have the two of you decided to do since the bureau won't annul your marriage?"

Casey's question reeled his thoughts back in. "Do what they want and live together for thirty days," he said.

"That's asking a lot of the two of you. Maybe you ought to seek out the advice of an attorney," Casey said.

"We thought of that, but in the end it might only delay things," he said, and his conversation with Jared last night had only confirmed his suspicions. "Alyssa thinks it will work since she's able to do her job from anywhere. She's a Web site designer."

"Um, maybe you can get her to design the Web site for Uncle Sid's foundation that we're setting up," Casey suggested.

"I mentioned it to her briefly, and you're right. It might be something she can do while she's here if she has the time."

"She'll be at the ranch when McKinnon and I visit in a few weeks," Casey said as if thinking out loud. "I'm looking forward to meeting her."

Casey's intonation immediately sent up red flags. He knew his sister. After that Chantelle fiasco she had gotten a little overprotective where he was concerned. He found it rather amusing although not necessary. "Don't forget who's the oldest, Casey," he decided to remind her.

Over the phone line he heard her unladylike snort. "But only by a mere fourteen minutes. I would have been the oldest if it wasn't for Cole holding me back."

Clint laughed. That's the reason Casey liked telling everyone for her being the last born. She had gotten that tale from Chester, who had convinced her she was in position to be born first. "Whatever. Look, Case, I have a lot of work to do around here today. I'm expecting another shipment of horses," he said.

"Wonderful. McKinnon and I will talk with you later to let you know the exact day we'll be arriving."

Moments later Clint ended the call with Casey thinking that she was usually a good judge of character. He wondered what she would think of Alyssa.

Seven

Alyssa glanced around Clint's office thinking how the one in her home was a lot smaller. She loved her small apartment. It was just the right size for her. All she needed was a kitchen, bedroom, bath and working space. She had considered the living and dining rooms as a bonus.

She studied the different pictures on the wall and recognized the one of Sid Roberts. Another showed a woman with three little ones—about the age of five or six—at her side. She knew that it was a picture of Clint, his mother and two siblings. There was another framed photograph of his mother alone. She was beautiful and Alyssa could easily see Clint's resemblance to her; the likeness seemed very strong. She thought that Clint favored his mother until she saw yet another photograph of a man she immediately decided had to be Clint's father. Any resemblance she'd attributed to his mother dimmed when she compared the image of Clint she had in her mind to the picture of his father. Clint had his father's domineering features. Both Clint and Cole, whose looks were nearly identical, had inherited their father's forehead, chiseled jaw and matching dark eyes. They had also inherited their dad's sexy lips, the lips that she loved to look at on Clint. The father, whom Clint said he'd only met a few years ago, definitely was a good-looking man. Alyssa quickly formed the opinion that Casey, although she had her father's eyes, had inherited more of her mother's features.

Alyssa tensed when she heard her cell phone ring. She had recently gotten a new number and hoped that Kim hadn't gotten hold of it. Flipping the phone open, she smiled when she saw it was her aunt calling. "Yes, Aunt Claudine?"

"Just wanted you to know that I got those boxes shipped off like I said I would. You should get them in a few days."

"Thank you. I appreciate your going to the trouble," Alyssa said.

"No trouble. Kim dropped by this morning trying to sweet-talk me into telling where you were. I didn't tell her a thing. Actually, I told her you were off seeing a client."

"Thanks, I appreciate it," Alyssa said.

"Jessie also called asking about you, but I figured Kim put him up to it."

Alyssa had to assume the same thing. Her uncle rarely sought her out these days.

"And how are things with you and your cowboy?"

Alyssa chuckled. "He isn't my cowboy, but things are going just fine." At least she hoped they were. She hadn't seen him since breakfast that morning. She knew he had returned for lunch because she had heard him when he'd ridden up on his horse. She had glanced out the window—being careful not to be been seen this time—and watched as Clint dismounted and walked with his horse toward the stables. The way the jeans hugged his body nearly took her breath away.

"I'm glad to hear it. Well, I've got to go. Eleanor is dropping by later and we're going to attend a church function together later."

"Okay, Aunt Claudine, and thanks for everything," Alyssa said.

"You're welcome."

Alyssa hung up the phone thinking how appreciative she was of her aunt.

"How are things going?"

She turned to see Clint standing in the doorway.

"They're going fine. My aunt is shipping some boxes to me and I'm hoping to get them in a few days," Alyssa said.

Opening her mouth and getting words out had been a real challenge, especially with the way he was looking at her. Heat was beginning to slither through her body from the intensity of his gaze. He stood leaning in the doorway and she could feel her control begin to unravel.

Whether she liked it or not, desire seemed to grip her each and every time she saw him.

"In the meantime," he said, interrupting her thoughts, "I figured you might need some additional clothing so I placed a few items of clothes on your bed."

She lifted a brow. "Clothes?"

"Yes."

"Women's clothes?" There was a suspicious note in her voice which she wished wasn't there. She further wished he wouldn't pick up on it.

"Yes, women's clothes. You and Casey are about the same size so I took the liberty of borrowing some of her things for you. When she left for Montana she wasn't certain she would be staying so she left some of her things here," Clint said.

Alyssa felt relief that the clothes belonged to his sister and not some other woman. She was mature enough to know that Clint had probably dated a slew of women over the years. Some had probably stayed at the ranch. That was his business. And what he did after the thirty days were up and their marriage was annulled was also his business. *So why did the thought that his business could include other women bother her?*

And then there was the thought that he had been in her bedroom. Granted, this was his house, the one he'd grown up in as a child, which meant that he probably knew the location of every room blindfolded. But the idea that he had been in the room where she'd slept last night, had gotten close to the bed, made every nerve in her body tingle.

"Thanks for being so thoughtful," she managed to say as she stood.

"No problem."

When it became obvious that he had no intention of leaving—he just stood in that same spot staring at her—she raised a brow.

"Is there something else?"

"Yes, there is," he said.

She felt the lump in her throat. She didn't want to ask but felt compelled to do so anyway.

"And what is that?"

"Chester wanted to know if you would be joining us for dinner," Clint said, clearly uncomfortable with extending the invitation to her.

Alyssa released another deep sigh as she studied his expression. That hadn't been what she expected him to say and she felt a touch of unwanted disappointment. It had been her idea that they agree on how far they would take their attraction, so why was she feeling so edgy?

"Alyssa?"

"Yes?"

"Will you be joining us?"

She wondered if he really wanted her to.

"And how do you feel about me joining you for dinner, Clint?" she asked quietly.

He rubbed his chin as he continued to look at her. She watched as his gaze slowly scanned her body from head to toe. He smiled slightly and then said, "We're having meat loaf. I'd much rather look at you across the table than down at a plate of meat loaf." He added, "Chester usually burns it. He says it's supposed to taste better that way."

She couldn't help her smile. "Does it? Taste better that way?"

"Not really," he said, looking thoughtful. "But then the only taste I seem to enjoy lately is yours."

His words singed fire through her body with the force of a blowtorch. A woman could only take so much flirting with a man like Clint. She watched as he slowly moved away from the door to walk toward her. And as if her feet had a mind of their own, they moved, and she found herself coming from around the desk to meet him. He came to a stop right in front of her and his eyes stared into hers.

"This is crazy. You know that, don't you?" As he asked her that question, he leaned forward and circled her waist with his arm. The heat of his words warmed her lips.

"Yes. Real crazy," she heard herself mumbling in response.

"I'm going to be real pissed about it later," he said, catching her bottom lip between his teeth for a gentle nip. "But right now, at this minute, I have to taste you again."

And then as if to prove his point, when she tilted her head up to him he reached out and gently took hold of a section of her hair and tenderly pulled her mouth closer to his, locking it in place. He was determined to take the kiss deeper. Make it even more intimate.

She didn't think that was possible until she felt the tip of his tongue coaxing hers to participate. Hers gave in and together they explored every sensitive area of her mouth. Her senses went on full alert and she became a turbulent mass of longing. In all her twenty-seven years, it had taken a trip to Austin to discover what it meant to be kissed senseless.

The kiss seemed to go on nonstop and Alyssa felt herself being passionately consumed with a need that was making her feel weak. It just didn't seem possible that within days of seeing Clint again after five years, she could be this attracted to him.

He pulled back and ended the kiss, but not before gently nipping at her bottom lip as if she was a tasty morsel he just had to have. And then he took his fingertip and traced it across her wet and swollen lips. "You did want my kiss, didn't you?"

She didn't answer immediately, and then she decided to be totally honest with him. "Yes, I wanted it. But—"

He quickly swooped down and captured her mouth with his again, and she hungrily opened her mouth beneath his. Yes, she had wanted it and he was making sure she was getting it.

This time when he pulled back he placed a finger against her lips to make sure she didn't utter a single word.

"No buts, Alyssa. I know my limitations. I'm aware of the terms that I agreed to. The only person who can renege on them is you," he said.

Arousal was shining in his eyes and she could feel his erection pressed hard against her stomach. "And if you ever decide to do so," he added in a husky tone, "you're fully aware of where my bedroom is located. You are more than welcome to join me there at any time."

"Are you sure Alyssa will be joining you for dinner?"

Clint first glanced at the clock on the stove before meeting Chester's gaze. "That's what she said, but who knows, she might have changed her mind."

Chester stood leaning against the counter and held a spatula in his hand. He narrowed his eyes at Clint as he placed his arms across his chest. "What did you do to her?"

Clint rolled his eyes. "I didn't do anything to her. I merely told her that—"

"Sorry I'm late," Alyssa said as she rushed into the kitchen.

Both men's gazes shifted to Alyssa. Clint's gaze went from her to Chester's accusing glare. *If you didn't do anything to her then why are her lips all swollen?* the old man's expression seemed to say.

Instead of cowering under Chester's glare, Clint stood and returned his gaze to Alyssa. "No harm done. Besides, you are worth the wait," Clint said.

And he meant it. She was wearing one of Casey's outfits that he'd placed on the bed for her. Funny thing was, he never remembered Casey looking that good in the sundress.

"Thank you," Alyssa said.

She crossed the room to take her place at the dining room table—space usually reserved for the lady of the house. Clint wondered if she knew that. He sat down as she began easily conversing with Chester, asking how his day had been at the hospital. While setting everything on the table, Chester told her of how one of the kids had been afraid of him and how he had finally won the child over by doing magic tricks.

"Will the two of you need anything else before I go?"

"Where are you going?"

"I'm going to the bunkhouse to feed the ranch hands," the older man said and smiled.

"Oh," Alyssa said. "No, I won't need anything else."

"Neither will I," Clint tacked on, more than ready for Chester to leave the two of them alone. He had heard the catch in her voice letting him know that the thought of being alone with him made her nervous. She should be nervous, Clint thought. Whether she knew it or not, she was driving him crazy. If the outfit she was wearing wasn't bad enough, her scent was definitely getting to him, almost drugging his senses, eating away at his control. The sundress had spaghetti straps and revealed soft, creamy flesh on her arms and shoulders. It was skin he ached to feel, touch and taste. He would love to trace his tongue along her arm and work his way up to her shoulders and—

"Clint, Chester is saying something to you," Alyssa was saying.

He blinked at her words and then sent a sharp glance in Chester's direction. The old geezer had the nerve to smile as if he knew where Clint's thoughts had been.

"What?" Clint probably asked the question more roughly than he should have, but at that moment, he really felt like he was losing it.

The older man's smile widened when he said, "I was trying to get your attention to remind you that I won't be here in the morning. Snuggles the Clown is doing another performance at the hospital."

"I remember," Clint said shortly.

"Oh, by the way, Alyssa offered to do breakfast for the men in the morning," Chester said, undeterred by Clint's sour expression or gruff tone.

Clint shifted his gaze from Chester to Alyssa. "You did?"

"Yes. It's the least I can do around here," Alyssa said.

Clint frowned. "That's a lot of food to prepare. Nobody said you had to do anything around here," he said.

"I know, but everyone around here has chores. Fixing breakfast tomorrow will help me to feel useful," she replied.

"What about the work you were doing on the computer for that client?" Clint was not sure he liked the idea of her in his kitchen performing domestic tasks. There hadn't been a woman in his kitchen since Ada died.

"I'm almost done and on deadline," Alyssa said, smiling proudly.

Clint leaned back in his chair. "Well, let me know when you're ready to take on another customer. I was serious when I mentioned I needed a Web site for the Sid Roberts Foundation."

She lifted a brow. "And you want me to do it?"

"Only if you have the time. The next time you're in my office take a look in the side drawer on your right.

There's a folder with information about the foundation in there. If you decide to do it, we can sit down and discuss it when I get back," he said.

"Get back? Are you going someplace?"

He heard the catch in her voice again. "I'm not going off the property so I'll still be safe in saying we were together for the thirty days, but I'll be spending a couple of nights under the stars on the south ridge. The horses arrived today and the ones I've decided not to train I'll be setting free on that designated land that's governed by the foundation," Clint said.

"And how long will you be away from the ranch?"

He shrugged. "It usually takes a couple of days."

"Oh," Alyssa said.

"Well, folks, I'll be leaving," Chester said. Clint shot the older man a glance. He'd forgotten he was still in the room. He had been too focused on Alyssa and that wasn't good.

"So, did you get a lot accomplished today?" Clint asked as he loaded his plate with food.

Alyssa watched him and was again amazed at the amount of food he consumed. "Yes, I put in a lot of time doing that Web site. It's for a teachers' union in Alabama."

He nodded. "How do you get your clients?"

"Word of mouth mostly. One satisfied client will tell another. But I'm also listed in all the search engines and that helps," she said.

"I take it that you're good at what you do," Clint said.

She glanced up and met his gaze. She hoped they were still talking about the same thing. "Yes, I'm good. I believe in satisfying my customers and I rarely get complaints. If you need references then I can—"

"No, I don't need references."

Conversation between them ceased again, which was fine with her since he seemed keen on eating his meal. She wondered if he still thought the taste of the meat loaf had nothing on her. It was hard to tell since he seemed to be enjoying every bite of it. But then whenever he kissed her it appeared that he tried to gobble her up, as well.

"Is something wrong?"

She blinked. "No. Why?"

"You're staring. You have a tendency to do that a lot when we eat together. Is there a reason why?"

Alyssa shifted in her seat. There was no way she could tell him that she found watching him eat fascinating…and a total turn on. He seemed to appreciate every piece he put into his mouth. And the way he would take his time to chew it, methodically getting all he could from each bite, let her know he would make love to her the same way. Given the chance, Clint would savor her in the same way that he ate. Goose bumps formed on her arms at the thought of it.

"No reason," she said after pausing for a moment to gather her thoughts. "It's just that I'm totally in awe of how much you eat."

He lifted a brow. "And I'm in awe as to how little you eat. You remind me of Casey. She eats like a bird, as well," he said.

She heard the fondness in his voice for his sibling. "I appreciate your sharing her clothes with me. I hope she won't mind," she said.

"She won't," he said, effectively closing discussion on the subject. "Will you be using the computer later?"

"No," she said, shaking her head. "I'm through for the day. I thought I might look through that folder you were telling me about on your uncle's foundation. Why?"

"Because I need to use it to log in the information on the horses we got in today," he said. He glanced at his watch as he pushed his plate aside. It was clean. "I play cards with the men on Wednesday night so I'll be leaving the house again after logging in that information. And I won't be back until way after midnight," he said with a smile. "I'm telling you this just in case you want to play another game on the computer later. I promise not to interrupt you this time."

"This is your house, Clint. You have free rein of any place in it."

He cocked his head and looked at her. "Even your bedroom?"

The glint in his eyes indicated that he was teasing her. At least she hoped he was.

"No. According to our agreement bedrooms are off-limits," she said.

"Um, that really doesn't bother me. The bedroom is one of the places I least like for making love," he said slyly.

She suddenly felt like she was under the influence of some sort of drug. Sensations were surging through her, touching all parts of her body, but especially the area between her thighs.

"What is your favorite place?" she couldn't help asking.

Alyssa stared as he put his glass of lemonade down. His gaze was intent on holding hers. She tried fighting it but she was being pulled into his sensuous web.

He smiled and that smile, like his words, touched her all over. It added kerosene to her already blazing fire. "Before the thirty days are up," he said in a deep, throaty voice, as his gaze held hers, "I intend to show you."

An hour or so later Alyssa stood at her bedroom window and watched as Clint walked across the yard to the bunkhouse, which meant his office was empty again. She needed to think and wanted a quiet place to do so. His office was the perfect place.

The man was getting to her in a big way and he was doing so with a degree of confident arrogance that astounded her. He wasn't pushy or demanding. He wasn't even using manipulating tactics. He was merely being his own sexy self.

Before the thirty days are up, I intend to show you.

Those words were still ringing in her ears, still causing an ache in parts of her body that aches had never invaded before. The area between her thighs was actually throbbing. Clint had basically assured her that he would make love to her at some point before she left his ranch. Such a statement was bold, bigheaded…and heaven help her, probably true.

She inhaled sharply. *How could she of all people, someone who rebuffed men's sexual advances with mediocre kindness, even contemplate such a thing happening?* She was not only contemplating it, Alyssa was actually anticipating it.

She shook her head to clear it, needing to focus mainly on the facts. Clint Westmoreland was the sexiest man she had ever seen in clothes, so naturally a part of her—the feminine part—couldn't help wondering what he looked like without clothes. That kind of curiosity was new for her.

Then there was the way Clint carried himself. He had a self-assured nature that was very attractive. And lastly, she couldn't downplay the fact that since meeting him, she experienced an all-consuming desire that had invaded her entire body. It wasn't in her normal routine to lust after a man but she was definitely lusting after Clint Westmoreland.

She turned away from the window, her mind stricken by what she was thinking, her body shaken by what it needed. The couple of times she had made love with Kevin, it hadn't done anything for her. She hadn't felt the earth shake and she hadn't experienced the feeling of coming out of her skin. In fact, she had been inwardly counting the minutes when it would be over. Was it possible an experience with Clint would be just the opposite? Would it be one she wouldn't want to end? Such thoughts made her draw in a shaky breath.

As she crossed the room and slipped between the cool covers of the bed, she had a feeling that sleep wouldn't come easily for her tonight, especially since the aches in her body wouldn't go away.

By the time she finally closed her eyes, she was convinced that dreaming about all the things Clint could do to her wasn't sufficient. She wanted to experience the real thing.

Eight

The next morning Alyssa entered the kitchen to find Clint already sitting at the table drinking coffee. She frowned. She had hoped to get up before him and have breakfast started.

"Chester said he usually doesn't start cooking until around five o'clock. You're up early," she said, glancing at him while going straight to the sink to wash her hands.

A smile touched the corners of his lips as he shrugged one broad shoulder. "I thought I'd have a cup of coffee while watching you work," he said.

She raised her chin defiantly. "You don't think I can handle things?" Alyssa asked in an accusing tone.

"Oh, trust me. I believe you can handle things. Chester wouldn't let you in his kitchen if he thought otherwise. I just wanted to watch you do it and offer my help if you need it," he said.

"Thanks."

"Don't mention it."

A short while later Alyssa wondered if she'd been too quick to give Clint her thanks. Each time she moved around the kitchen she felt his eyes on her and had a feeling his intense stares had nothing to do with her culinary skills. She was dressed in another of the outfits belonging to his sister. This one was a pair of jeans and a top. He'd been right. She and Casey were about the same size and so far everything she'd tried on fit perfectly.

She turned around from the stove to tell him that everything was ready and her gaze collided with his. She saw something flicker in the dark depths of his eyes and that fiery light sent a burning sensation through her middle. She swallowed the lump in her throat. "Everything is ready."

Then, following Chester's instructions, she called the foreman at the bunkhouse to let him know the meal was ready to be picked up. She had prepared enough food to feed at least fifty people and was grateful for all those times she had helped Aunt Claudine and the other older ladies at church prepare meals for the homeless.

She hung up the phone only to find Clint standing only inches away from her and her pulse rate escalated. He was the epitome of handsome and radiated a sex appeal she couldn't deal with this early in the morning.

"You did an outstanding job," he said, and the sound of his voice only added to her discomfort. Alyssa began to feel a tingling sensation all over.

She tried playing off the feeling. "Save your compliment until after you've tasted it," she tried saying lightly.

He smiled. "Don't have to. I watched you. You definitely know your way around the kitchen."

She chuckled. "Thanks to Aunt Claudine, I would have to agree. I helped her out with feeding the homeless at least once a week. I never thought doing so would come in handy one day," she said heartily. "It felt good doing it. Chester has everything so well organized. This kitchen is a cook's dream."

"And you, Alyssa Barkley, are a man's dream," he said in a low voice.

He leaned forward and she knew he was going to kiss her. Just then she heard the sound of footsteps on the back porch. She took a step back.

"The guys are coming for the food," she said softly.

"So I hear," he said silkily and took a step back, as well. He glanced at his watch. "It's time for me to go, anyway."

"You're not going to stay and eat breakfast?" she asked quickly, before she could stop herself. Alyssa prayed he hadn't heard the disappointment in her voice.

"I'm going to eat with the men in the bunkhouse before leaving." And then before she could blink, he had recovered the steps and placed a tender kiss on her lips. "I'll see you in a couple of days."

Alyssa nodded, thinking she could definitely use two

days without him hovering about. She would have two full days to get her head screwed back on right.

That first day Alyssa was still convinced that distance was just what she needed from Clint. She was glad he would be away from the ranch. Once her boxes had arrived, she'd taken the time to unpack. Her aunt had sent her everything she needed, from an adequate supply of clothes for the chilly days of February yet to come, to a sufficient supply of underwear.

By the second day Alyssa found herself glancing out the window wondering if perhaps Clint would return a day early—even though she tried to convince herself that she really didn't want him to. She enjoyed her talks with Chester and a few of the ranch hands who had remained behind.

On the third day, Alyssa paced the floor in his office when she couldn't sit still long enough to work at the computer. And every time she heard a commotion outside the window she found herself racing toward it to see if it was Clint returning. By late evening after sharing dinner with Chester, she found herself standing on the front porch staring out into the distance. She was reminded of a woman standing on the shore waiting for her man to return from the sea. The comparison struck her. For the first time since coming to Austin, she began to realize that her emotions were getting too deep. It was becoming obvious to Alyssa that she was developing feelings for Clint.

She sighed deeply, knowing it didn't make sense.

They had been reunited just days ago. The only excuse she could come up with was that Clint Westmoreland—with his arrogant confidence and untamed sensuality—was more virile than Kevin could ever hope to be. She hadn't been involved with a man since that fateful day—her wedding day.

Finding out Kevin had been unfaithful had been a blow, but what had been even more of a shocker was the very idea that he felt they should forget what he'd done and move on. She couldn't move on. Instead she had sought to protect her heart from further damage the only way she knew how—avoid any personal dealings with men. She had responded in just the way Kim had counted on.

Alyssa had long ago accepted that her cousin didn't want her to be happy and didn't want Alyssa to have a man in her life. The thought of Alyssa having a man who loved her, who wanted to give her his world and his babies was something Kim was determined to prevent.

She knew Aunt Claudine was right when she would say that she needed to move on and not give Kim the victory. But she hadn't met a man worthy of such a task…until now.

Clint Westmoreland made her want to take a chance on living again in a way she had denied herself for almost two years. And even if it was only for the time she stayed on his ranch, she knew that she wouldn't have to worry about Kim being around to sabotage her relationship with Clint. Alyssa was smart enough to know that any relationship that she developed with him wouldn't last. At the end of the thirty days he would want her gone, off his ranch and out of his life.

In the past, Alyssa had avoided casual relationships, but for some reason she didn't see the time that she would spend with Clint as a casual fling. It would be more than that. Indulging in pleasure seemed a fitting term for their relationship. She considered her feelings for Clint a reawakening. If she had an affair with him, it would be a way to rebuild her self-esteem and regain her confidence as a woman. It would also be a way to enjoy life before returning to the mundane existence she'd carved out for herself in Waco.

"Nice night, isn't it?"

Alyssa was pulled out of her reverie when Chester walked out onto the porch. She was discovering each and every day just how much she liked the older man. He was loyal to Clint and his siblings to a fault and she liked that. It reminded her so much of how her relationship with her grandfather had been and the relationship she shared with her aunt now.

"It is a nice night," she said simply. She knew he was perceptive enough to figure out why she was outside standing on the porch in the dark and his next statement proved it.

"Sometimes it takes longer than the two days to set free the horses. Some of them can get real frisky when they are taken out of their element. I bet the reason Clint hasn't returned yet is because he'd had his hands full."

Alyssa sensed that Chester was telling her that Clint hadn't been staying away from the ranch just to avoid her. *How had Chester known that was exactly what she had been thinking?*

Alyssa smiled as she pulled the jacket she was wearing more tightly around her shoulders. February was proving to be a colder month than January.

"Clint said that your grandfather used to be a bronco rider," Chester said.

"Yes, he was. In fact that's how he met Sid Roberts. It was an experience he took pride in telling me about while growing up."

"You were close to him," Chester said.

"Yes, he was the most special person in my life."

Less than an hour later when getting ready for bed, Alyssa remembered those words and knew in her heart that Clint was becoming a special person to her, as well.

Clint almost weakened as he gazed down at a sleeping Alyssa. A stream of light from a lamppost poured into her window and illuminated her features. He wasn't sure what she was wearing under the bedspread because her body was completely covered, but she looked incredibly sexy.

Okay, he had broken their agreement and had come into her bedroom. He'd done so because Chester had told him that she had stood outside on the porch that night waiting for him to return.

At first Clint hadn't wanted to believe it, but then a part of him realized that the possibility existed that she had indeed missed him…like he had missed her. Clint stiffened at the thought that he could miss any woman, but whether he liked it or not, he had. And she had constantly invaded his dreams since she'd come to the ranch. He didn't like that, either.

How could she get to him so deep and so quickly? He'd had other women since Chantelle, but none of them had made a lasting impression. None of them had even come close. But Alyssa was making more than a lasting impression. She was carving a niche right under his skin and it got deeper and deeper each and every time he saw her.

He studied Alyssa when she made a sound in her sleep. A lock of her hair and fallen onto her face. He leaned down and brushed the tendril back, careful not to wake her. He sighed knowing he had no right to be there, but also knowing that he would not have been able to sleep a wink if he had not looked in on her. He also knew his presence in her bedroom was about more than that. It was about wanting to be close to Alyssa.

He hated knowing how much he had wanted to see her and be with her. Clint fervently hoped that by the morning he would have regained control of the situation. He had to get whatever emotions he was battling in check and start putting her at a distance.

He frowned as he turned to leave the room and contemplated his plan of action with difficulty. It would mean more days spent away from the ranch. That had been his plan in the beginning. *Then why did the thought of following through with his original strategy leave such a bitter taste in his mouth?*

Upon awaking the next morning, Alyssa heard a group of men talking not far from her bedroom window.

She got out of her bed and slipped into her robe before crossing the floor to the window and glancing out. Her heart nearly stopped beating. The three men she saw were among those who had left the ranch with Clint, which could only mean he had returned, as well. She couldn't help the smile that covered her lips as she headed for the bathroom.

Less than thirty minutes later she was dressed and eager to get down to breakfast before Clint left for the day. She felt a burning desire to see him, come face-to-face with him and get all into his space. She looked at herself one last time in the mirror before she left the room. She didn't look bad in her jeans and shirt, she thought with a smile. She also wore the new boots she had purchased the day before yesterday when she'd caught a ride into town with Chester. Alyssa felt like a bona fide cowgirl.

She breathed in deeply and with shaking hands she reached to open her bedroom door. Alyssa hoped that by the time she made it to the kitchen her heart would no longer be beating so wildly in her chest. It would be a struggle to keep it together knowing Clint was back and they would be once again breathing the same air.

She opened the door to step out into the hallway and her heart caught. Standing there, leaning against the opposite wall as if he'd been waiting for her, was Clint. Alyssa was speechless. And before she could open her mouth to utter a single word, he moved from the spot, pulled her into his arms and kissed her, devouring her mouth with an urgency that astounded her.

Alyssa sagged against him and wrapped her arms

around his neck as his mouth and tongue continued plundering hers. She didn't think about struggling to keep herself together or trying to gain any semblance of control of the situation. The only thing she could think about was that he was back. He was here. And he was taking her mouth with a hunger that meant he had missed her to the same degree she had missed him. That thought made her giddy.

Everything was forgotten. How she had intended to protect her heart from further damage, and how she had decided at some point during the night to retreat back into her hands-off strategy. All her concentration was on the intense arousal overtaking her belly as she kissed Clint with the same fervor and passion that he was kissing her.

And then when he finally released her mouth, he didn't let go of her lips. He took the tip of his tongue and outlined a sensuous path from one corner to the other, over and over again. Alyssa heard herself groan. She actually felt her panties get wet. Clint had the ability to reach down, deep inside of her, to a place no man had gone for two years. He was stirring up a need, one as intense as anything she had ever encountered.

"I've got to go," Clint whispered against her moist lips. The deep, raspy tone of his voice knocked down the last reserve of strength she was trying to hold on to.

"Breakfast?" she asked. The only word she could get her lips to form.

"I've already eaten. I need to be on that back pasture. I'll be gone all day and wanted to see you before I left. I wanted to taste you."

His words made every single cell in her body multiply with excitement. Then, as if the kiss they'd just shared would not be enough to sustain him through the day, he took hold of her mouth with lightning speed once more. She returned the kiss. She hadn't been aware that she was so starved for such male interaction until now, but not interaction from just any male. She wanted it only from Clint.

When he finally released her mouth she knew her lips would be swollen again. Anyone seeing her would know why, but at the moment she didn't care.

"I have to go," he said again, and as if fighting the urge to take her into his arms yet again, he stepped back. He stared at her for a long moment before reaching out and gently touching her swollen lips with his fingertips. "I promised myself last night that I wouldn't do this," he said in a low, throaty voice. "But I can't seem to help it. You, Alyssa Barkley, are more of a temptation than I counted on you being."

Without giving her a chance to say anything he turned and she watched him walk away.

"Hey, boss, are you okay?" one of Clint's men inquired some hours later as he was saddling one of the horses.

Clint glanced up at Walter Pockets, frowned and said gruffly, "I'm fine. Why do you ask?"

The man, who had only been working for him a couple of years, hesitated. "Well, because you're putting the saddle on backward," he said.

"Damn," Clint said and quickly removed the saddle.

He placed it on the horse's back correctly, grateful that only Pockets had seen him make such a blunder. "My mind was elsewhere," he said. He knew that was a lame excuse. He would be the first to get on his men if they were to let their minds wander while performing even a menial task. Working on a ranch required focus. And yet, he was not focused at all today.

"I can ride out and check on things if you want me to," Pockets said.

Clint thought about the man's offer. It was almost lunchtime already. He had pretty much decided to stay out on the range and eat with his men, but now he was thinking differently. Kissing Alyssa had not gotten her out of his system. Instead it seemed that each time their lips connected she was getting even more embedded under his skin. Yet he could no more seize an opportunity to kiss her than he could stop breathing.

"Thanks, Pockets," he finally heard himself say. "I'd appreciate it if you would. I've got a matter up at the house I need to take care of." That was saying it as honestly as he could.

Less than thirty minutes later he was walking into the kitchen. Chester glanced up from stirring a pot with a surprised look on his face. "I didn't expect you back until late tonight."

Clint shrugged. "I finished early. Where's Alyssa? Is she in my office?"

"No, she asked if she could borrow the truck to go into town. She said she was going to take a shower, so I guess she's in her bedroom getting dressed."

The thought of a naked Alyssa standing under a spray of water got him even more unfocused and aroused and he was grateful to be standing behind the kitchen table. Wondering why Alyssa needed to go into town, Clint headed toward his office.

"Maybe you ought to think about going with her," he heard Chester say. Clint drew up short and turned around.

"Why should I think about doing something like that?"

Chester smiled. "Because you could help her with all those bags and boxes she plans to bring back."

Clint frowned. "What bags and boxes?"

"From shopping. I figure she's going into town to do some shopping," Chester said.

Clint folded his arms over his chest. "Why in the hell would I want to accompany any woman shopping?"

Chester chuckled. "That would give you a chance to spend time with her under the pretense of being helpful. And don't insult my intelligence by asking why I think you'd want to spend time with her, Clint. I saw her lips at breakfast."

Clint's frowned deepened. "And?"

"And I think you need to go easy on them," the older man said with a sly chuckle.

Clint honestly didn't think he could. Instead of telling that to Chester he turned and walked out of the kitchen.

"Where are the keys to the truck, Chester?" Alyssa asked, glancing around. She could have sworn when Chester had given them to her earlier she had placed them on the top of the breakfast bar.

"Clint has them," Chester said.

She whirled around with a surprised look on her face. "Clint?"

"Yep," Chester answered without looking up from stirring the pot on the stove.

"Oh. I thought he was going to be gone all day," Alyssa said.

The older man did manage to smile. "Yeah, I thought so, too, but I guess he had a change in plans."

"Does that mean he needs to use the truck?"

"No," Chester said, chuckling. "I think it means that he's going into town with you."

Alyssa swallowed the lump in her throat. "Are you sure?"

"Positive. In fact he's waiting outside for you," Chester said.

Alyssa knew she looked startled, but Chester wouldn't know because he didn't seem to be paying attention to her. He was focused on his cooking.

"Well, I guess I'll see you in an hour or so," she said, glancing at her watch.

"Don't count on it," Chester said.

"Excuse me?" she responded, not sure she had heard Chester correctly.

"Nothing," the older man said.

Alyssa eyed Chester in confusion, certain that he had said something. However, instead of questioning him further, on wobbly legs she headed toward the living room to leave. *Why would Clint want to accompany her into town? Had he gotten a call from Hightower? Surely he would have told her if he had.*

She stopped short of opening the door, needing to pull herself together. This would be the first time she saw him since their morning kiss. It was a kiss from which she still hadn't fully recovered. And she had assumed that since he would be away from the ranch all day and she wouldn't see him again until tomorrow at the earliest, that she would have time to compose her senses.

Taking a deep breath, she opened the door and saw Clint standing in the yard. He was leaning against his truck and her stomach became filled with butterflies when she realized that he was waiting for her.

She was careful walking down the steps, trying not to trip. She was amazingly aware of the appraisal he was giving her with his dark, intense eyes. He was looking her up and down, from the top of her head to the toes of her booted feet.

She decided to return the favor and check him out, as well. She saw that he'd taken the time to shower and change, too. He looked good enough to eat leaning against the truck in a pair of jeans and a blue chambray shirt. His legs were crossed at his booted ankles and he wore a black cowboy hat on his head. He was the epitome of sexy, the essence of what she definitely considered a fine man and the personification of everything male.

As she walked up to him she saw desire in his eyes and she took a misstep. He reached out and caught her arm and brought her closer to him. The front of their bodies touched and his lips were mere inches from hers.

"Are you okay?" he asked in a low, husky tone.

She wanted to tell him that no, she wasn't okay, and she wouldn't fully recuperate until she left his ranch for good. In the meantime, for the first time in her life she was beginning to think about all the things she could get into while she was there. And when she left, she would have solid, red-hot memories to hold on to during the night while lying in her bed alone. "Yes, I'm fine," she finally managed to say.

In response, as quick as a cricket, he swiped his tongue across her lips just seconds before releasing her. She blinked, not sure he'd done it until she felt the wetness he had left behind.

"Ready to go?" he asked in a husky voice, transferring his hold from her arm to her hand. The feel of his touch had her heart thudding in her chest.

"Yes, I am," she said.

He opened the truck door for her and she slid inside. He stood there a moment and she wondered if he was going to kiss her again. He leaned closer but instead of kissing her he snapped the seat belt into place around her hips.

"Thanks," she barely managed to get out.

He smiled. "No problem." And then he straightened and closed the door.

With almost stiff fingers she clutched her purse as she watched him walk around the front of the truck to get inside while whistling a tune she wasn't familiar with. Then he was buckling up his own seat belt and starting the engine. "Where to?" he looked over and asked her.

Her eyebrow arched. He definitely seemed to be in a good mood. "You're taking time away from your busy schedule to be my personal chauffeur," she said as a grin touched lips that were still warm and wet from his kiss.

He grinned back. "I guess you could say that. When I heard you were going to do some shopping in town I decided that now was a good time to get that new belt that I need."

"Oh." But that didn't explain why he was back at the ranch when he had mentioned that morning he would be gone all day. Alyssa decided it really didn't matter why he had altered his plans. He had and she was glad about it.

"So where to first?" he asked her again.

"What about the Highland Mall?" she asked. That particular mall had been her favorite when she lived in Austin as a Ranger.

"The Highland Mall it is."

She settled back in her seat, anticipating how the rest of the day would pan out.

Nine

It was late afternoon before Clint and Alyssa returned to the ranch. In addition to shopping, Clint had suggested they see a movie. He could tell that Alyssa had been surprised by his suggestion. There were ten movies showing and they had narrowed their selections down to two. They couldn't decide which of the two to see, so they ended up viewing both.

Clint had enjoyed Alyssa's company immensely. He'd discovered several new facets of her character. For instance, Alyssa loved Mexican food and she was thrilled about her work as a Web designer. During the course of the day, she'd explained the process of setting up a Web site and how each design was tailored to the individual needs of each client. She'd also gone into detail about search engines and how invaluable they were to anyone who frequented the Internet.

They ate lunch at the mall food court and he had enjoyed watching her eat every single bite of her meal. In fact, he had gotten turned on just from watching her eat. *Was that crazy or what?*

And another thing that was crazy was that he had enjoyed being with her while she shopped. In his opinion, she was a smart shopper. He had definitely learned a lot today about working a clearance rack.

"So where do you want these bags and boxes?" he asked as he followed her into the house.

"You can carry them into my bedroom."

He glanced over at her and grinned. "Is that an invitation?"

She shook her head and grinned back. "You may enter my bedroom this time, but only to deliver my packages, Clint."

As they walked together down the wide hallway that turned off into the wing where she was staying, a part of him regretted his decision to make sure the guest room she used was so far from his bedroom.

"Did I tell you how nice you look today?" he asked softly as they neared her bedroom.

She glanced over at him. "Thank you."

He could tell his compliment had caught her off guard. When they reached the bedroom, he stood back while she led him in. "You can place everything on the bed."

"Sure," he said. He had come into the bedroom last night while she had slept and the memory of seeing her so relaxed and at peace sent sensations of desire spiraling through him now.

After placing the items on the bed, he turned and saw her watching him. And there it was again. He had felt it all day around her—the spark, sizzle and steam that seemed to emanate between them. He knew she was aware of it, too.

"I believe this one is yours," she said, retrieving a single bag from the bed and offering it to him.

"My belt," he said and chuckled.

He took the bag and then gently pulled her to him. He saw the flicker of passion in the depths of her eyes. "I always say I'm not going to kiss you and end up doing it anyway," he said.

"Why?"

A smile touched his expression. "I've told you why. Do you want me to remind you?"

"Yes, why not?" she teased.

He leaned into her, let her feel the evidence of his desire that was pressed hard against her. He spread the palms of his hands at the center of her back, bringing her closer to the fit of him. "Should I say more?" he asked in a voice that sounded deeper to his own ears.

She held his gaze. "Yes, say more," she said daringly.

He leaned over and licked her cheek with the tip of his tongue. "I like tasting you and one of these days, Alyssa, I plan on tasting you all over."

He heard her sharp intake of breath. He was being blunt, but he was also being truthful. Things couldn't continue between them at the rate they were going.

They hadn't made it to their second week together and already things were almost sizzling out of control. Hadn't Chester just today hinted that he should go easy on her lips? As if he ever really could.

"Remember our agreement," she said in a quiet voice.

"I remember it," he said, still holding her close. "Do you?"

She tilted her head up and looked at him. "Yes, I do."

"You're the one who initiated this, Alyssa, and you're the only one who can finish it. I will adhere to our agreement as long as you want me to," he said.

"B-but what about all these insinuations you're making?" she whispered accusingly.

He smiled, thinking about all he had said. "What about them?"

She studied his features and then evidently decided he wasn't serious. "You're teasing me," she said.

"No," he said. "I'm not teasing. I'm dead serious."

As if tired of what she perceived as his game-playing, she lifted her chin and said, "You can't have it both ways, Clint."

He laughed although his features were without humor. "Sweetheart, when I finally have you, I plan on having it in ways I've only recently dreamed of." And as if to prove his point, his thighs moved at the same time he pressed gently in the curve of her back to bring her closer to him.

He then leaned down and placed a gentle kiss on her lips and felt himself harden even more. "I'll see you at dinner."

"I'm skipping dinner tonight," Alyssa replied.

"Not because of me, I hope," he said in a low tone.

"No," she said tightly. "Because of me."

Alyssa stretched out on the bed. It was nearly midnight. She had taken a shower and changed into one of many oversize T-shirts she enjoyed sleeping in.

Good to her word, she had skipped dinner because she needed to be away from Clint. She had called her aunt earlier and they had chatted awhile. Luckily, Aunt Claudine hadn't asked her anything about Clint and Alyssa had had no reason to bring him up.

Chester had knocked on her door earlier to make sure she really didn't want anything to eat and had even offered to serve dinner to her in her room if she preferred. She had assured him she was fine and she wasn't hungry. She figured Chester thought the reason she was missing dinner was because of a tiff she'd had with Clint, which wasn't the truth. She just needed distance from him right now. He had the tendency to prevent her from thinking straight. He would say things with such conceit that he rattled her confidence. He seemed so sure of her when she wasn't sure of herself, she thought.

Her cell phone rang and she frowned wondering who would be calling her at this hour. Aunt Claudine was usually in bed by nine. She sat up and reached for the phone. Her frown deepened when she saw the caller indicated Kim was on the line. She wondered how Kim had gotten her number. There was no way Aunt Claudine would have given it to her.

"Yes?" She decided it was time to stop avoiding her cousin.

"Well, well, for a moment I thought you had dropped off the face of the earth," Kim said.

Alyssa rolled her eyes. "What do you want, Kim?"

"Where are you?"

"It doesn't matter to you. What do you want?"

"Everyone is wondering where you are. You just took off without telling anyone," Kim said smartly.

"I did tell someone," Alyssa replied.

"Yeah, we figured Aunt Claudine knew where you are but she isn't talking. All she's saying is that you left town to go visit a client."

"Whatever," Alyssa said, sidestepping Kim's attempts to get more information.

"Really, Alyssa, don't you think it's time for me and you to sit down and have a little chat? I'm sick and tired of you blaming me because you can't keep a man. It's not my fault that they end up finding you inadequate and prefer me to you," Kim said.

"Look, Kim, I have to go."

"And you're not going to tell me where you are?"

"No."

"Suit yourself."

"I will. Goodbye and please don't call back." Alyssa then hung up the phone.

Inhaling deeply, she swung her legs off the bed as she fought back the anger she felt. Overconfident people were wearing on her nerves, although she had to admit that Kim was very different from Clint. She couldn't imagine Clint ever deliberately hurting anyone. Deciding she needed to work off some of her negative energy, she decided to slip into Clint's office to play a game on his computer.

It was late and chances were he was in bed asleep by now. At least she hoped so. She opened her bedroom door and, as expected, the entire house was quiet. She appreciated the night-lights that lined the hallway as she made her way from her wing toward the one where Clint's office was located. As far as she knew, they were the only ones living in the main house. Chester lived a few miles away in a house on land Sid Roberts had willed to him.

Alyssa slowly opened the office door and found the room empty. She quickly moved across the room to Clint's desk. Kim's words had put her on edge. She was still fuming while waiting for the computer to boot up.

She turned when a knock sounded on the door. She went still when Clint walked in. Closing the door behind him, he leaned against it.

Alyssa tried not to let her focus linger on his dark eyes, but when she moved her gaze to his strong jawline and kissable lips she realized she was in trouble looking there, too. She returned her gaze to his.

"I thought you were asleep," she said when she finally found her voice.

A smile touched the corners of his lips. "As you can see I'm very much awake."

Yes, she could definitely see that. She could also see in his nonchalant stance against the door just how perfectly his jeans fit his body, and with his chambray shirt open past the throat, she got a glimpse of his hairy, muscular chest. But what really caught her attention was the area below the belt. Not only was Clint very much awake, he was very much aroused, as well.

The thought that he wanted her was enough of a reason for her heart to pound and her pulse to drum. If that wasn't bad enough, her lips began tingling from remembered kisses. She already had a number of them tucked away in her memory bank.

She swallowed deeply as desire began to thrum through her and felt her body automatically respond to his. "Is there a reason why you're here?" she asked, hearing the slight quiver in her voice.

"Yes," he said in an arrogant tone as he moved away from the door and slowly strolled toward her.

From the glow of light off the computer screen she was conscious of every single thing about him, including the dark pupils in his eyes and the faint growth of stubble on his chin.

When he reached the edge of the desk he placed his hands palms down as he leaned closer and brought his face mere inches from hers.

"Tonight," he whispered against her lips, "I want to teach you another version of Playing with Fire."

Alyssa slowly backed away. She then tilted her head and looked up at him. "You agreed," she reminded him in an accusing voice, one she could barely force past her lips.

"I agreed not to seduce you into my bed, Alyssa," he

said. He momentarily released her gaze to glance around the room. "There's not one bed in here," he said.

She tilted her head a half inch higher. "You don't need a bed to do what you want to do. You've said so yourself," she said defiantly.

He smiled. "Yes, I did say that and it's true," he said in a husky voice. "To make love to you I don't need a bed. But you'll have to be willing, Alyssa. I would never force myself on you."

She believed him. But she also knew it wouldn't take much coercing on his part right now. He had become her weakness.

"I won't do anything you don't want me to do. Come play with me," he said throatily. "Trust me," he added as he offered her his hand.

The look in his eyes stirred her in a way she would not have thought possible and without realizing she was doing so, she began leaning toward him. And when she reached out and placed her hand in his, she knew she had literally sealed her fate.

Clint Westmoreland was demanding more of her than she had ever shared with any man. She was taking a risk, opening her heart up in a way she had never done with Kevin. And as she continued to gaze into the turbulent darkness of his eyes she suddenly knew why. Not only did she trust him, she had fallen in love with him, as well.

She was not going to waste her time wondering how it happened, or why it had happened. She was willing to accept that it had happened...just as she was willing to accept it would be a one-sided love affair that would lead nowhere. At the end of the thirty days she would be leaving. But at this very moment, she had tonight and wanted to take full advantage of it.

"I do trust you, Clint," she finally said softly. "Teach me how to play your game."

Ten

Still holding her hand in his, Clint moved around the desk to gently pull her up from her seat and into his arms. He knew she had to see the desire flaring in his eyes, had to know from his aroused state just how much he wanted her. And he did want her and had from the first, when he'd seen her at the airport.

Leaning slightly, he took the liberty to place his open hands over her bottom, bringing her closer to him, and groaned through clenched teeth when he felt her softness come to rest against his hardness. Desire ripped into him, adding to the heat that was already there.

"Alyssa." He moaned her name just moments before covering her mouth with his, devouring with an intensity that shook him to the core. He'd become familiar with her taste, the very essence of her flavor, and each time his mouth was reacquainted with it, one part of him wanted to savor it slowly, while the other part wanted to devour her whole.

He was too far gone to savor yet he refused to be rushed. He wanted to make their passion something she would enjoy. That way she would let him make love to her again…and again…and again.

In his mind, nothing about their relationship had changed. They were just taking things to the next level. They were adults and they would be able to handle it. They would make no promises, just pleasure. In thirty days, their marriage would be annulled and Alyssa would leave. His life would continue just the way it had before getting that fateful letter from the bureau. For some reason the thought of Alyssa leaving made him feel uneasy.

She pushed against his chest so he could release her mouth and when he saw her lips he understood why. Already they looked thoroughly kissed. “Don’t know just how much of that I can handle,” she whispered, trying to catch her breath.

He knew he could kiss her in other ways and was anxious to explore those options with her. In his mind, the game of playing with fire was basically doing just that, and he was curious to see just how much heat she could handle.

“Come with me,” he said as he led her over to the sofa. He sat down and then pulled her down in his lap. Immediately, he brushed a feathery kiss on the top of her head. When he saw her trying to pull the T-shirt she was wearing down to cover her exposed thighs, he stilled her hands.

"Don't," he whispered.

He reached out his hand to stroke her flesh there, liking the feel of her soft skin. From that first day he had enjoyed looking at her legs. But lately she had covered them up with jeans. The jeans she wore always emphasized her womanly curves, so he'd had no reason to complain, until now.

In fact, when it came to Alyssa, he was unable to find fault with anything. The only thing that gave him reason to pause was her unwillingness to discuss her family at any great length. He had tried getting her to talk about them while they were at the mall, but she hadn't had a lot to say. He couldn't help but wonder what they thought of her living with him for thirty days. Had she told them the full story like he had told his siblings? he wondered.

Cole had called earlier tonight from Mexico where he'd been for the past month on assignment. Like with Casey, Chester hadn't wasted any time sharing the news. It didn't come as a surprise that Cole had thought the situation rather amusing. Cole said he was glad it was Clint caught in that predicament and not him. Cole had claimed that he was too much of a ladies's man to be tied down to just one woman. The first question his brother had asked was if Alyssa was pretty. Clint had assured him that she was.

"Are you sure you don't want to keep her around?" Cole had asked.

Clint's response had been quick and resounding. "I'm positive. At the end of the thirty days she's out of here."

"Clint?"

The sound of Alyssa's voice pulled him from his reverie. He realized his hand had moved higher on her thigh. He smiled when he answered her. "Yes?"

"What are you going to do to me?" she whispered, tilting her head back to look at him.

In an amazingly calm voice, he said, "I'm going to introduce you to another version of Playing with Fire, but the object of the game will remain the same. My goal is to blow you up and, baby, I'm about to make you explode all over the place."

He murmured the words against her lips and felt them quiver beneath his. He then shifted her position in his lap to remove her T-shirt and wasn't surprised to find her completely naked underneath her nightclothes. She said she trusted him; now he would see just how much.

He stood with her in his arms and then laid her back on the sofa, fully open to his view. His gaze slid over her, lingering on her breasts, the gold ring in her navel, her womanly core and her long, beautiful legs.

"You are beautiful," he whispered, barely able to get the words out. Entranced, fascinated and totally captivated, he slowly dropped down to his knees in front of her, needing to touch her, taste her all over.

He reached out and his fingers immediately went to her breasts, cupping them in his hands before leaning closer to let the tip of his tongue taste the curve of her throat. Then he pulled back and watched his fingertips swirl around a budded nipple, feeling it pucker beneath his touch.

A soft moan escaped her lips and he saw she had closed her eyes, was biting on her lower lip. Little did she know he hadn't even gotten started.

"How does my touch feel, Alyssa?" he asked in a low voice as he continued drawing circles around her nipples with his fingertips.

"Good," she murmured in a voice so low he could barely hear her.

"Do you like it?"

"Yes," she responded and it seemed her words had been an effort. She refused to open her eyes to look at him.

He then slowly moved his hands, lowering them to her stomach, skimming the taut skin there. She felt soft to the touch and he smiled at the ring in her navel.

He eased his hand between her open thighs and heard her sharp intake of breath when he nudged her thighs even farther apart, wanting to touch and explore her everywhere. His fingers dipped inside of her. She was wet, drenched, and her scent consumed him totally.

Fighting the urge to taste her, he removed his hand from her and let his fingers travel downward past her knees and then to her beautiful feet. There wasn't a part of her he wanted left untouched.

"Now for the taste test," he whispered, determined to taste Alyssa's first orgasm on his lips.

She opened her eyes and stared at him. "I don't think I can handle much more."

He smiled. "You can. Trust me."

She nodded and he leaned forward and captured her nipples in his mouth. And things started from there. Never had he wanted to taste a woman so badly, and he went about showing her how much. She looked so sensual and sexy that intense emotions tore into him as he moved his mouth lower to the area he craved.

She let out another deep groan the moment he lowered his head between her legs, and when the tip of his tongue touched her she nearly came off the sofa. But he had no intentions of letting her go. He pulled back only long enough to shift her body to place her legs over his shoulders. He was filled with a primitive sexual energy that was consuming him. He intended to transfer that energy to her in this very intimate way.

He tightened his hold on her hips and lowered his mouth to her and immediately found his mark, capturing her womanly core, locking his mouth to it. She tasted sweet. She released a litany of moans and arched her back and he greedily began tormenting her with his tongue.

Her body was on fire, he could feel it. She was on the verge of exploding. He could feel that, as well. His grip tightened on her hips when she let out a scream and he continued to hungrily stroke her with his tongue, enjoying the way she was pushing her body against his mouth.

God, she was responsive, completely filled with passion, a fantasy come true. And when she couldn't take any more and blew up, when an explosion racked her body, he continued to give her a hard kiss. He felt his own loins about to burst and fought back for control. This was her time. His time would come later.

Tonight was for her.

When the last quake left her body, he pulled her into his arms and kissed her. He would give her time to recover and then he intended to perform the process all over again.

Sitting across the room at his desk, Clint's gaze encompassed Alyssa, who was knocked out on his sofa. He smiled, thinking that too much passion could definitely do that to a person. Deciding he wanted to let her sleep but didn't want to leave her alone, he decided to pass the time browsing the Internet.

First he checked out the Web site that advertised her company and was impressed with what he saw and the listing of references. Her clients consisted of both corporations and a mom who was using the site to organize a carpooling network.

Deciding to use one of those search engines she had told him about at lunch, he was able to locate several foundations that had a similar goal as the Sid Roberts Foundation—saving wild horses. One such organization was located in Arizona. Reaching for a pen, he jotted the information down. He would contact the organization the next day.

Then with nothing else to do, he decided to search Alyssa's name. Perhaps such a search would list other Web sites that she'd done or was associated with.

In addition to bringing up several sites that her name was linked to, he was also given a list of news articles in which her name appeared. One was an article about an award she had received for Web design. A semblance of pride touched him at her accomplishment.

Then his gaze sharpened when it came across another article. It was one that announced her marriage engagement. Clint instantly felt a sharp pain that was similar to a swift kick in his abdomen. Alyssa hadn't told him she'd been engaged.

He flipped to the another article and his breath caught at the headlines that read Attorney Kevin Brady Weds Alyssa Barkley.

Clint's shoulders stiffened but he managed to force them to lean forward in his chair as he read the article that was dated two years ago. "In the presence of over five hundred guests, prominent Waco attorney Kevin Brady wed local Web designer Alyssa Barkley." There was also a picture of a beautiful Alyssa in a wedding gown.

Clint flipped off that particular screen, angered beyond belief at the thought that there was a possibility he had just made love to someone else's wife. During their very first conversations the day she'd arrived in Austin, Alyssa had told him she was not married. Yet the article indicated that she had been married. Even if she had gotten a divorce, she should have told him about it. This changed everything, Clint thought angrily.

Stunned, he stood and moved away from the computer, feeling let down and used. Taking the chair on the other side of the sofa, he decided not to wake her. So he waited until she finally awakened a half hour later. He watched as she slowly opened her eyes, saw him sitting in the chair and smiled at him. He could tell by her expression that she was confused by his refusal to return her smile.

"Clint?" she asked, pulling her naked body up into a sitting position. "What's wrong?"

He didn't say anything as he tried to ignore her nudity before she reached for her T-shirt and pulled it over her head. Then in a voice tinged with the anger he was trying to hold in check, he asked, "Why didn't you tell me you had gotten married, Alyssa?"

Eleven

Alyssa went stiff. From Clint's expression she knew he mistook the gesture for guilt. A part of her immediately wondered if it mattered what he thought since he had been quick to think the worst of her, to believe she could be married to someone and willingly participate in what they had shared tonight. Her anger flared. *Just what type of woman did he think she was?*

But then she knew what he thought did matter. What he had done tonight, not once but twice, had been intense, passionate and an unselfish giving of himself.

"I asked you a question, Alyssa," Clint said in the same hard voice.

Reining her anger back in and holding his gaze, she shook her head. "I'm not married, Clint."

"But you were," he said.

It wasn't a question, it was an accusation. She wondered where he had gotten his information. It would seem like the handiwork of Kim, but she knew that couldn't be the case.

"Alyssa," he said.

Apparently she wasn't answering quickly enough to suit him. The details of the humiliating day of her wedding were something she didn't like remembering, much less talking about. Having all those people at the church know the reason she hadn't gone through with the wedding—that she had been unable to satisfy her future husband to the point where already he'd gone out seeking the attentions of others—had been a degrading experience for her.

Knowing Clint was waiting for a response, she lifted her chin and tilted her head and slanted him a look.

"I've never been married, Clint," she said.

She saw his anger die down somewhat, but she also saw the confused look in the depths of his dark eyes.

"Then explain that picture and this article on Internet," he said.

So that was where he'd gotten his misinformation, she thought. With as much dignity as she could muster, Alyssa sat up straight on the sofa.

"The wedding was supposed to take place, but it didn't and it was too late to pull the article scheduled to run in the newspaper. To be honest, I didn't even think about calling the papers to stop the announcement from printing the next day. I had other things on my mind," Alyssa said.

Like how my cousin could hate me so much to do such a thing, and how my fiancé, the man I thought I loved, could allow her to use him to accomplish such a hateful act, she thought.

"You're saying that you called things off on your wedding day?"

She heard the incredulous tone of his voice as if such a thing was paramount to the burning of the flag. "Yes, that's what I'm saying," she said.

She knew that statement wouldn't suffice. He needed to know more. So she began talking and remembering that dreadful day. Her feelings of shame and embarrassment hadn't lessened with time.

"I was home that day getting ready to leave for the church when a courier delivered a package for me. It contained pictures of my soon-to-be husband in bed with someone I knew. The pictures arrived just in time to ruin what should have been the happiest day of my life," Alyssa said.

She watched Clinton's fury return, but this time it wasn't directed at her.

"Are you saying that while engaged to you your fiancé was sleeping around? And with someone you knew and that the person deliberately wanted to hurt you?"

She nodded. "Yes, and the pictures were very explicit. Kevin didn't even really apologize. He said he felt his behavior was something I should be able to forgive him for. He said I should get over it because it just happened that one time and meant nothing."

"Bullshit," Clint said.

Alyssa tried not to smile. "Yes, that's what I said."

"And the woman involved?"

"She accomplished her goal, which was to hurt me and embarrass me. She wanted to prove that there was nothing that I considered mine that she couldn't have," Alyssa said.

He frowned. "She doesn't sound like a very nice person."

She thought that over for a moment. "In my opinion, she's not."

The room got quiet and Alyssa was very much aware of him staring at her, so she tried looking at everything else in the room but him. She wondered what he was thinking. Did he agree with some of the others who'd pitied her because they felt she hadn't been able to hold on to her man, keep him from wandering?

She heard Clint move and when she glanced over in his direction she was startled to find him standing in front of her. She lifted confused eyes to his. When he reached out his hand to her, she took it and he gently pulled her to her feet and off the sofa. Instantly, his arms went around her waist and he pulled her tighter to him.

"I just made a mistake in accusing you of something when I should have checked out the facts first," he said, in a low, husky tone. "I'm sorry and I can assure you that it won't happen again," he said, holding her gaze with his.

"And I'm glad you didn't marry that guy because if you would have married him, you wouldn't be here with me now." A few moments later he added while placing his palm against her cheek, "Besides, he didn't deserve you."

That's the same thing her aunt had said that day. Over the years, Claudine had just about convinced Alyssa that it was true. Touched by what he'd said, Alyssa tilted her head back and slanted a small smile at him. "Thank you for saying that," she said.

"Don't thank me, sweetheart, because it's true. Any man who screws around on a woman like you can't be operating with a full deck."

Alyssa shrugged. "You haven't seen the other woman," she said.

"Don't have to. Beauty is only skin deep and a real man knows that. I'm not the kind to get taken in by just a pretty face," Clint said and he smiled down at her. "Although I would be the first to admit that you do have a pretty face," he added in a husky voice. "Come on. Let me walk you to your room."

She drew in a deep breath thinking how quick and easy it had been to fall in love with Clint. Even now, when she knew he didn't feel the same way, she loved him so deeply it made her ache. It also made her want to express her love in the only way she knew how, and with the time limit they had, the only way she could.

"We didn't finish the game," she said softly, remembering the two orgasms he had given her and how she had passed out before returning the favor.

He reached out and gently caressed her bottom lip. "No, we didn't, but you've had enough for one night. We'll play again at another time. Trust me."

She did and it suddenly occurred to her at that moment just how much.

* * *

Alyssa woke up the next morning overwhelmed that in just one night things had changed between her and Clint. There was no doubt in her mind that he still expected them to annul the marriage and for her to return to Waco at the end of the thirty days. But then, she thought, smiling, there was also no doubt in her mind that he wanted her the way a man wanted a woman. He had proven as much last night.

She glanced over at the clock and quickly sat up as her heart jumped in her chest. It was just before eight in the morning. Clint was an early riser. On most mornings he was up and out before six. She wondered if she had already missed him.

She slid out of bed and moved quickly to the bathroom to take a shower, remembering his hands and mouth on every part of her body. Moments later in the shower and under the spray of warm water, she glanced down and saw the marks of passion his mouth had made on her skin. Most of them, like the ones on her stomach and thighs, could be easily covered by her clothes, but the ones on her neck were blatantly visible. They would be hard to hide. At the moment she didn't care.

A short while later she'd finished dressing. She'd decided to wear a new pair of jeans she had purchased the day before and a top she had picked up while at the mall. Sighing deeply, she left the bedroom, hoping Clint was still around and hadn't left the ranch for the day.

"Is there any reason your eyes are glued to that door?" Chester asked, chuckling. Clint didn't answer.

"Hey, give her a while. She'll be coming through that door at any minute. Unless your wife has a reason to sleep late this morning," Chester teased.

Your wife.

Clint felt his stomach roll into a knot. It was only when he was conversing with Chester that Clint remembered that legally Alyssa was his wife. As his spouse, she was as deeply embedded as any woman could get in his life.

"*Does* she have a reason to sleep late, Clint?"

Chester's question broke into his thoughts. He didn't bother glancing over in Chester's direction because he had no intention answering the old man. Yes, Alyssa had plenty of reasons to sleep late this morning and all of them involved what they had done in his office last night. He got hard just thinking about their "game" and was grateful he was sitting down and away from Chester's prying eyes. The old man saw way too much to suit Clint.

"Clint, you're not answering my question."

Clint's gaze remained glued to the door that separated the kitchen from the dining room. "And I don't intend to, Chester. Don't you have work around here to do?"

"Don't you?"

Clint frowned. He did have plenty of work to do and he was getting behind in it if the truth was known. But he needed to see Alyssa. All through the night he thought about what she had shared with him about her unfaithful fiancé and her horrible wedding day. Her revelations had nagged at him to the point where he'd been unable to sleep.

He then recalled how he had found out about Chantelle's infidelity. When she believed his future aspirations did not include anything else other than being a Texas Ranger, Chantelle had sought out greener pastures and had married a banker.

Clint knew all about betrayals. He knew how it felt to believe you were in love with someone and believe that person loved you back only to have that love tarnished with treachery.

Somewhere in the house he heard a door close and the sound snapped him out of his thoughts. He glanced over at Chester. "Don't you have the men to feed?"

Chester chuckled. "I've fed them already, but if that's a way of asking me to get lost, then I'll take the hint," he said, wiping off his hands with a kitchen towel. "Lucky for you I can come back and clean this stove later." The older man smiled over at Clint before grabbing his hat off the rack and turning toward the back door.

Before reaching it Chester turned around. "Have you given any thought to attending the annual benefit for the children's hospital I was telling you about? This year it will be held at the governor's mansion. Important people from all over Texas will be there. I reminded Casey about it. The function will happen during her visit, and she and McKinnon have agreed to go.

"And I even took the liberty to contact some of your cousins. Most of them said they would fly in to attend. Wasn't that real nice of them?"

Chester paused only long enough to add, "I haven't

gotten a firm commitment from Cole or you, though." He chuckled. "At least this year you won't have a problem getting a date since you have a wife."

Clint shot Chester a glare before the man turned around to open the back door. Chester was barely out of the door when Clint stood up, immediately dismissing what Chester had said from his mind. The man was becoming a smart-ass in his old age.

Clint heard steps and felt his stomach clench in anticipation. He was eager to see Alyssa. Ready. Eager. Waiting. The kitchen door swung open and then she was there. Smiling at him. And she looked so damn good in a pair of jeans, shirt and cowboy boots. Her thick, copper-brown hair flowed around her shoulders, framing her gorgeous face. She looked prettier than anything or anyone he had seen in a long time.

"Good morning, Clint," she said.

Without responding, he walked around the table and pulled her into his arms and whispered, "Good morning, Alyssa." He leaned down and captured her lips, needing to taste her again, to have her in his arms, to be consumed by her very essence. He didn't understand what was happening to him and at the moment, he didn't want to analyze his feelings or scrutinize his actions. The only thing he wanted to do was what he was now doing, exploring Alyssa's mouth with a hunger that astounded him.

He finally raised his head and gazed down at her moist lips, and when she whispered his name he leaned down again for another taste as pleasure tore through him. It was the kind of pleasure that licked at his heels, filled him with a warm rush and had certain parts of his body aching for relief.

This time when he pulled back again he placed a finger against her lips. "I love kissing you," he whispered.

She smiled sweetly. "I figured as much, especially after last night."

He smiled. "Come on, let's feed you. Chester kept your breakfast warm."

"And yours?"

"I've already eaten, but I'll join you at the table and drink another cup of coffee while you eat."

"All right," Alyssa said.

He took her hand and led her to the table thinking that he could definitely get used to her presence in his home.

She melted a little bit inside each and every time Clint glanced her way. A couple of times he had looked at his watch. She knew he had work around the ranch to do, but he was putting his work aside for her. But she didn't want to keep him from doing his job.

"I got a chance to read all that information about the foundation and the reason for it," she said, to break the comfortable silence between them.

He took a sip of his coffee as his intense gaze still held hers. "Did you?"

"Yes. And I got some wonderful ideas for the site that I would like to share with you. That is if you were really serious about my doing a web design for it," she said.

"Yes, I'm serious. I've even spoken to Casey about it," Clint assured her.

She raised a brow. "You have?"

He chuckled. "Yes. I'm president and executive director of the board that consists of my brother and sister. We've hired several others to work with us who are just as determined as we are to relocate as many horses as we can. We also want to educate the public to the plight of the wild horses," Clint said.

She nodded. "I guess all three of you love horses."

He grinned. "With a passion, and speaking of horses, I want you to have all your work done by three o'clock today."

She lifted a brow. "Why?"

"Because you and I are going riding," he said.

She frowned. "If you recall, I told you I'd rather not get on a horse," Alyssa said.

"I recall, but riding a horse is just like riding a bike. If you take a fall you get back on and try again."

"Even if you break your arm in the fall?"

"Yes, even if you broke your arm. How old were you when it happened?"

"Ten," she said.

"Ten? Then it's definitely about time we do something about conquering your fear about riding. So, do we have a date at three?"

"Yes, we have a date," she said with a smile.

Twelve

Alyssa took a deep breath as she stepped out on the front porch. Like the day before, Clint was in the yard waiting for her. This time he wasn't leaning against his truck. Today he was sitting on the back of what Alyssa perceived as the largest horse she'd ever seen. The big black stallion was beautiful, although he looked very mean.

"He won't bite," Clint said.

She glanced up at Clint, not at all certain. "Are you sure about that?"

"Positive. I wouldn't let anything harm a hair on your head. I thought I'd start you off easy. Today you'll ride with me. Royal can handle the both of us."

"Royal?"

"Yes. He was the first stallion we brought from

Nevada last year. He was very wild and unruly," he explained.

She grinned. "And of course you tamed him."

"I did. And he's been my horse ever since," Clint added with pride.

She looked at the fierce-looking animal and then back at Clint. "Evidently you're good at what you do."

"I'm not perfect. I make my share of mistakes, but thanks," he said. "Now come closer so I can lift you up."

Ignoring the way the horse was looking at her, she went closer so that Clint could hoist her up onto the horse's back. He effortlessly pulled her up to sit behind him. She gripped her arms tightly around his waist.

He glanced over his shoulder at her. "Ready?"

"As much as I'll ever be. And you promise I won't fall off?"

He smiled. "I promise," he said.

Satisfied with his answer, she rested her chest against his back. "Then, yes, I'm ready," she said, trying to sound brave.

And she held on as Clint trotted for a few moments around the yard. And then when they reached the wide, open plain, he took off and she held on to him for dear life.

Clint liked the feel of Alyssa holding on to him as they continued their ride. He knew where he was taking her. Clint had a special spot on his ranch and he wanted to share it with Alyssa.

"You okay back there?" he asked her. She hadn't said much since they had left the ranch.

Instead of answering right away, she tightened her arms around him and snuggled even closer. He could feel the hardened tips of her breasts against his back. He could tell she wasn't wearing a bra and it felt good. And the way her thighs were squeezing him as she tried to grip the horse's sides turned him on.

"Yes, I'm fine," she finally said. "Where are we going?"

"You'll see," he said over his shoulder. "We'll be there in a minute."

As if satisfied with his response, she continued to hold on and together they rode against the wind.

It didn't take them long to get to the south-ridge pasture and he brought Royal to a stop near a thicket of oak trees. Dismounting, he took the horse's reins and securely tied them to a tree. He then glanced up at Alyssa, who was sitting demurely on the animal's back, and thought she looked totally incredible. Thick desire flowed through his bloodstream as he looked at her.

He walked back over to the horse and lifted his arms to help her dismount. The moment their bodies touched, fire blazed his loins and more than anything, he wanted to kiss her right there, under the beautiful blue sky.

And so he did.

He took her mouth with a hunger that always astounded him, and when she offered him her tongue, he greedily devoured her. The sounds of her moans ignited his cells. She continued to kiss him back and every stroke of her tongue was sure, refined and totally into what she was doing.

He pulled back. It was either that or else be tempted to take the kiss all the way. He hadn't brought her here for that. He had wanted to show her something, share something with her. "Come here," he said, grabbing hold of her hand and leading her toward the edge that looked down into a valley.

She followed his gaze and he knew she saw what he was seeing. Down in the valley there were thousands of wild horses running free. "Clint, this is truly magnificent," she said.

He glanced over at her, continued to hold her hand. "That night while you slept and I was on the computer, I looked up several other foundations that are similar to the one we started for Uncle Sid. Others have made it their business to save the horses, too."

A sound below caught their attention and they glanced down to see two horses that seemed to be at war with each other. "Stallions constantly struggle for dominance of their herd," Clint explained as they watched what was happening below. Two stallions were fighting it out, rearing up, biting and kicking each other. "Stallions go about gathering breeding mares into a band that they consider theirs," Clint said.

He chuckled. "Sort of like a harem, so to speak. And then they have the job of defending their band from other stallions who try to steal their mares. That's when there's fighting. The stallions are merely trying to hold on to what they consider theirs."

"So a herd only consists of a stallion and their mares?" Alyssa asked, seemingly fascinated by the information he was sharing.

"Eventually," Clint responded. "Once the mares give birth then the young foals stay with the band. However, once those young foals grow up and become young stallions they are chased away from the herd by the leader of the pack."

"What happens to them? The young stallions?"

"Usually young stallions gather together in their own herd—a bachelor band," he said and smiled. "They are fine until horniness sets in and then they go out looking for an available mare—which usually is in a band belonging to another stallion, and that's when more fighting takes place," he said.

"I understand horniness can be just plain awful," Alyssa said, smiling up at Clint.

"Yes," he agreed, returning her smile, knowing she was trying to tempt him. It was working. He pulled her to him, wanting her to feel just how much he desired her. "How about another game of Playing with Fire in my office later tonight?" he asked throatily.

She smiled up at him. "I wouldn't miss it."

When they returned to the ranch they were met by one of Clint's men, who said one of the wranglers had been thrown and was being rushed to the emergency room. Clint immediately went into action. Telling Alyssa that he would call her later, he got into his truck and took off.

While waiting for him to return, Alyssa tried to do

some work. She made notes on the proposal she would present to Clint and his siblings on the Web site design for the foundation.

Hours later, she stood and stretched her body. It was almost nine in the evening and Clint still hadn't returned. Nor had he called. Chester had assured her the young man had only broken a few bones and should be okay. Alyssa truly hoped he would be.

She almost jumped when she heard the sound of her cell phone ringing. Picking it up, she smiled when she saw it was her aunt Claudine. She was glad it wasn't Kim calling to harass her again. Her cousin hadn't bothered calling her back after that night.

"Aunt Claudine? How are you?"

She hadn't spoken to her aunt in a couple days so they spent the next hour or so catching up. When they finally ended their call, Alyssa decided to take a long and leisurely bubble bath.

A short while later after slipping into a T-shirt, she couldn't help but recall the words Clint had spoken to her a week or so before.

I know the terms of the agreement and the only person who can renege on them is you. And if you ever decide to do so, you're fully aware of where my bedroom is located. You are more than welcome to join me there at any time.

He had issued the invitation and now she intended to accept it. Walking out of her bedroom, she headed down the long hallway that led to the wing where Clint's personal domain was located.

When he came home tonight she would there, waiting for him.

* * *

Clint entered his house thinking hospital chairs were murder on a person's body. But at least Frankie would be okay. The kid was tough. He had a broken rib and collarbone to prove it. While at the hospital when he'd been trying so hard not to worry about Frankie, he allowed his mind to think about Alyssa. Clint hoped she hadn't been waiting for him in his office as he had asked her. He glanced at the large shopping bag that he was carrying. A display at one of the hospital's gift shops had reminded him that tomorrow was Valentine's Day. It seemed like years since he had purchased a card or candy for a woman, but tonight he had bought something for Alyssa.

Deciding the first thing he needed to do was take a shower, he entered his bedroom. The moment he opened the door, he picked up Alyssa's scent. A small table lamp provided a faint glow in the room and he quickly scanned the area. His breath caught in his chest when he saw Alyssa curled up in his bed.

He placed the gift bag in a chair and then went into the bathroom and closed the door to take a shower. She needed as much sleep as she could get now, because he fully intended to keep her awake for the rest of the night.

Alyssa was dreaming. Clint was in bed with her, caressing her stomach with his fingertips at the same time he was kissing her awake. But she refused to wake up for fear her fantasy dream would end.

"Alyssa."

She heard his voice and smiled dreamily at the way

he said her name. Dreams could seem so real at times, she thought....

"Wake up, sweetheart. I want you."

And then she realized it wasn't a dream. Alyssa felt Clint's very real, hot breath caress the words against her lips. She forced her eyes open and found his eyes holding hers. She was immediately pulled into their dark depths.

"You're home," she whispered sleepily.

"Yes, I'm home," he said.

And then he was kissing her with an intensity that shook her to the core, made her wet between the legs, filling her with a physical hunger that was just as intense as it had been the previous night. She became warm and tingly all over and she felt she was under some sort of sensual torture.

And then he pulled back from her lips and began using his tongue like he had last night—causing tiny little quivers to invade her body every place it traveled. First, he caressed her in the hollow of her collarbone, and then lower to her breasts. When he moved his mouth even lower, she gritted her teeth, refusing to scream out like she had last night. The effort was useless. When the tip of his tongue began greedily lapping the essence of her femininity, she lifted her hips off the mattress at the same time his name was ripped from her throat.

"Clint!"

And then she felt her thighs being nudged farther apart as he settled the weight of his body between them, and just seconds before her body exploded into a shattering climax, he entered her in one deep thrust.

She screamed again and arched her body as he continued to thrust powerfully into her, without any signs of letting up. Each stroke was with relentless precision that suddenly brought her to another climax. It was as if he couldn't get enough of her and the greedier he became, the more shamelessly she welcomed him, encouraging him to penetrate deeper.

Her nails raked his back and she bit him several times on the shoulder, but he refused to let up. A primitive need was driving him. The same need that was taking over her.

And then he shouted her name at the same time she felt the sensational buildup of his body coming apart on top of her. Together they shuddered as pleasure ripped through her in a way she felt all the way to her bones.

And while the last of the tremors vibrated through their bodies, he pulled her closer into his arms and kissed her tenderly. She knew how it felt to be consumed in passion, gripped in the clutches of desire and then to glory in the aftermath of fulfillment. The experience was simply priceless and she knew in her heart she would only be able to reach that level of satisfaction with him.

It was close to nine the next morning before Alyssa came awake to find she had spent the night in Clint's bed. A smile touched her lips when she remembered their night together. It was as if a searing need had taken over them and they had filled that need the only way they knew how. Sensations flooded her just thinking about it. Luckily for her, he'd been prepared and had used a condom. Birth control had been the last thing on her mind. They had made love several times, all through the night, and each time she reached an orgasm, he had been right there with her.

She lay on her back a moment thinking Clint would have had breakfast already and left the ranch, which meant she wouldn't get the chance to see him until later. She had a number of things to do today to stay busy. She slid out of bed thinking it was time to return to her own room when she noticed the huge red gift bag sitting on Clint's dresser with her name on it. She quickly crossed the room and pulled off the card.

Her heart caught at the single question on the card.

Will you be my Valentine?
—Clint

It then occurred to her that today was Valentine's Day. It had been years since she'd had a reason to remember it or for someone to give her a gift. Even while she'd been dating Kevin he hadn't bothered to acknowledge the day. His excuse was that he didn't need a designated day to give her something. Kevin had claimed the day was nothing more than a day for businesses to make money off gullible consumers.

She smiled. If Clint was a gullible consumer then she appreciated it because it really made her day knowing he had thought of her. She then looked into the bag and her smile widened when she saw among the tissue paper a box of chocolate candy and an oversize T-shirt. She chuckled when she read the wording on the shirt—I Like Playing with Fire.

She knew the shirt was a private joke between them.

She turned her attention back to her Valentine's Day card and smiled. She would definitely be Clint's Valentine, she thought. And set her mind to work on ways to make him hers.

It was almost ten that night before Clint returned to the ranch. He and his men had spent the majority of the day away from the ranch and he was glad to be back. He figured Alyssa would be asleep now and wondered if like last night she would be in his bed.

He also wondered if she had liked the gift he had left her. Conflicting emotions were running through him. She had been an itch he thought he would never be tempted to scratch. Now he was tempted beyond reason.

He opened the door to his bedroom and his gaze went to the empty bed. Immediately, he felt a sense of disappointment. Then his heart skipped a beat when he saw the note on his pillow. He quickly crossed the room. He picked it up and read the words Alyssa had scrawled on the paper.

Yes, I will be your Valentine.
Come to me. I am waiting.
—Alyssa

Clint had no idea how long he stood there, glued to the spot, rereading her message. And then with an insatiable thirst he knew that only she could quench, he quickly headed for the bathroom, already tugging his shirt out of his jeans. He would take a shower and then he would go to Alyssa, determined not to keep her waiting any longer than he had to.

Alyssa heard the soft knock on her bedroom door and her pulse began to race. She glanced around the room, hoping the lit candles weren't overkill, but she liked candles. She thought the lush vanilla fragrance that filled the air was nice. She hoped Clint thought so, as well.

She then glanced down at herself. Clint had seen her in enough T-shirts so she decided tonight would be different. She had borrowed the truck and gone into town and purchased this particular outfit to stir things up a bit. Not that she thought it took much to arouse Clint. He seemed capable of that feat just from looking at her at times, she thought with a smile. Alyssa wanted this night to be special.

She made it to the door on shaky legs and inhaled deeply before turning the handle. There he stood in the doorway and when desire flared in his eyes when he looked at her, she smiled knowing her outfit would be a big hit. They would definitely be playing with fire tonight.

My God, Clint thought as he stood there staring at Alyssa. She was wrapped up like a gift, in bright red wrapping paper with a huge white bow. How in the hell had she managed it?

As if reading his thoughts she said, "It wasn't all that difficult getting into it. But the only way it comes off is for you to *unwrap* me. Now that might be the hard part."

Not in his book, he quickly thought. *Unwrapping* her would be easy, especially taking off the big white bow which covered the essence of her femininity. Now that would definitely be a treat and not a challenge.

He swiftly entered the room, closing the door behind him. It was then and only then that he allowed his gaze to shift from her just long enough to glance around. He saw the lit candles and heard the soft music playing in the background. His gaze then returned to her.

He reached out, closed his hands around her waist, found the start of the ribbon and began pulling, watching before his eyes as she unwrapped. By the time he was able to pull off the bow, his body was hard and thick. He parted her thighs the minute the last piece of wrapping dropped to the floor.

The bed was not far away, but he doubted he would make it that far. Instead he went to the zipper of his jeans and took out his aroused member. Like last night he was prepared and had already put on a condom, not willing to take any chances. He knew to what degree he wanted her.

He lifted her onto him and entered her in one smooth thrust. It had been years since he'd made love to a woman in a standing position, but tonight he had no choice. He wanted Alyssa now.

He backed her against the wall as she wrapped her legs around him and tilted her hips for deeper penetration. And with another deep thrust he planted himself inside her to the hilt.

"You're some gift, sweetheart," he whispered as he began moving in and out of her. And moments later when he felt her come apart in his arms he followed her over the edge and they clung together, drowning in the waves of ecstasy as he murmured her name breathlessly. She clung to him and it took all he could do to continue to stand upright.

"Now for the bed," he said a moment later when he felt himself getting hard all over again. Every nerve in his body, every cell, seemed branded by her touch, the essence of her being. His senses suddenly became filled with an emotion he refused to accept. And as he crossed the room to the bed, he knew they were counting down the days together. These precious moments were meant to be savored.

Thirteen

The days passed so quickly that a part of Alyssa wished there was some way she could slow things down. But then she looked forward to each night that she spent in Clint's arms. Neither of them spoke about the short time they had left, although they were both aware that in less than a week their days together would end.

Everyone was looking forward to Clint's sister and her husband's visit. Chester was already preparing what he knew to be Casey's favorite foods.

"You're going to like Casey," Chester had said to Alyssa one day while she helped him prepare lunch for the men. "I'm glad she has McKinnon. He has definitely made her happy."

Chester seemed so sure of what he said that Alyssa

couldn't help but be happy for Casey. She would be able to spend the rest of her life with the man she loved. Alyssa knew that she wasn't to be so lucky. But at least she would have plenty of memories to sustain her.

She smiled. Clint had already warned her not to even think about not sharing his bed during his sister's visit. She knew Cole and some of Clint's cousins and their wives would also be visiting. Even Clint's father and stepmother were coming. They all were coming to attend the charity ball that would be held in the governor's mansion that weekend. To say the house would be filled to capacity was an understatement.

She knew that Cole and Casey already knew why she was there, but she couldn't help wondering how many of Clint's other relatives knew the reason for her presence. *Had he talked to them about it? Did his father know she and Clint were married?* She tried not to consider their circumstances as an embarrassing situation any longer. Besides, a part of her didn't want to worry about what other people thought about her relationship with Clint. Why should they hide their love affair? she wondered. They were lovers. She couldn't help but shake her head at the absurdity of it all. They were a married couple who were also lovers.

And on top of everything else, they were becoming close friends. Good to his word, Clint took her riding every day and now she no longer feared riding on a horse alone…as long as Clint was close by.

She glanced at the folder on the desk as she sat in Clint's office. The proposal she had worked up for the foundation was complete and ready to present to Clint and his siblings when they arrived.

If they liked her proposal and accepted it, she and Clint would still be in contact with each other, at least until she had the site up and running. After the site was operational, she would be available to maintain it. It was a service she offered to all her clients. She didn't relish the thought of having a continuing business relationship with Clint after their marriage was annulled. It would open her up for heartbreak if Clint decided to begin to date again.

She closed her eyes, not wanting to think of such a thing happening, although she knew that eventually it would. Clint was too good-looking a man not to have a permanent lady in his life. But then, according to Clint, his uncle Sid had died a carefree bachelor, although Chester was convinced Sid had an offspring out there somewhere. He recalled a woman once writing Sid telling him she had given birth to his son, but stating she didn't want or need anything from him. She'd merely felt it was the right thing to do to let him know. However, she hadn't provided a return address, which eliminated the chance of Sid finding out if the claim was true, or establishing a relationship with his child.

"Alyssa?"

At the sound of her name she immediately came out of her reverie and discovered the sound was coming from the intercom system. It was Clint. She stood and quickly crossed the room to the box on the wall and pressed a button. "Yes?"

"Where are you?"

She smiled. "In your office. Why?"

"I'm in the living room. I want you to come out and meet my sister and brother-in-law," Clint said.

A lump suddenly formed in Alyssa's throat. She was definitely nervous about meeting Clint's family, but knew she couldn't hide out forever.

"I'm on my way."

In less than a day Alyssa was convinced she totally liked Casey Westmoreland Quinn. And her husband, McKinnon, in addition to being knockout gorgeous, was a very kind person. Alyssa thought the two made a beautiful couple and it was very easy to see they were very much in love.

"You and I need to go shopping," Casey exclaimed to her the following morning at breakfast.

Alyssa's lips spread into a smile as she took a sip of her coffee. "We do?"

"Yes. You mentioned you don't have anything to wear to the charity ball this weekend and neither do I. Besides," Casey added as a grin spread across her lips, "that way I get to spend time with you without Clint hovering about. He seems to think I'm going to reveal some deep, dark, embarrassing secret about him from our childhood. He's really overprotective where you're concerned. I guess I should thank my lucky stars that the two of you are already married."

Alyssa frowned. Surely Casey knew her and Clint's marriage wasn't going to last forever. In fact they were merely biding time waiting until the day came where they could end it. Alyssa's thoughts were interrupted when Casey's cell phone went off.

"Excuse me, Alyssa, while I get this."

Alyssa stood from the table to refill her coffee while Casey answered the phone. Clint and McKinnon had left the ranch early that morning and weren't expected to return until dinnertime. Clint was eager to show McKinnon the most recent pack of wild horses that had been shipped from Nevada.

"Great! That was Spencer," Casey informed her, after she had finished the call. "He and Chardonnay just arrived and are at the airport. They should be arriving at the ranch within the hour."

Alyssa raised a brow. "Chardonnay?"

Casey smiled. "Yes, that's her name. Her family owned a winery in California and she was named after her grandfather's favorite wine."

"Oh."

"So we might as well wait and take Chardonnay with us," Casey said.

Alyssa then decided to ask, "Do you know who else is coming?"

"Shopping with us?"

Alyssa shook her head, grinning. "No, coming to the ranch to attend the charity ball this weekend," she said.

Casey looked confused. "Didn't Clint tell you?"

"Not really. He mentioned some of his family was coming, but he didn't say exactly who. I'm sure he mentioned it to Chester for him to get the guest rooms prepared, though," Alyssa said.

Casey frowned. "Never mind if he did mention it to Chester. You're the mistress of the ranch and he should have specifically told you. You shouldn't be hearing it secondhand. Men can be so fruity at times," Casey said.

From what Casey had just said, it was apparent she wasn't aware of the circumstances surrounding her and Clint's marriage. "It's not that Clint's fruity," Alyssa said, coming to his defense. "It's just that he doesn't consider me as the mistress of this ranch."

Casey raised a brow. "And why not?"

Alyssa sighed. If Clint hadn't informed his sister of anything, she wasn't sure it was her place to do so. She hesitated to find the proper words, couldn't find them, shrugged and then said, "Because he just doesn't."

Casey stared at her as if trying to figure out what she meant and then a smile touched her lips. "Oh, you're talking about that business with the thirty days and how the two of you have to live under the same roof and all of that?"

Alyssa nodded. *So Clint had told her*. "Yes."

Casey chuckled before taking a sip of her coffee. "I wouldn't worry about that if I were you. Trust me, Clint plans to keep you," Casey said.

Alyssa shook her head. "No, he doesn't," Alyssa argued.

Casey laughed. "Yes, he does and what's so sad is that besides being fruity, some men are also slow. Clint is one of the slow ones. Chances are he hasn't even realized what he plans to do with you yet, poor thing."

Alyssa stared at Casey, wondering how she could

make such an assumption. The only excuse she could come up with was that since Casey was happily married and in love she thought everyone should be the same way. Alyssa decided not to argue, and to let Casey continue to think whatever she wanted to believe. But Alyssa was fully aware of the real deal surrounding her marriage to Clint and that at the end of thirty days he expected her packed and ready to leave.

Two nights later Alyssa lay in Clint's arms after thoroughly being made love to. The sound of his even breathing let her know he had gone to sleep, but she was wide-awake…and thinking.

All of Clint's relatives who were attending tomorrow night's ball had arrived and she found all of them to be extremely nice and friendly. The house was full and without it being verbally expressed, Clint looked to her to be his hostess and instinctively she had taken on the role. When he introduced her, he simply said she was Alyssa. He didn't give her last name or what role she played in his life. She could only assume the masses thought she was his live-in lover since she wasn't wearing a wedding ring and it was obvious they shared the same bed. But what was confusing was that when the relatives talked among each other in her presence and his, she was referred to as Clint's wife and he did nothing to correct them.

She guessed in a way it didn't matter what they thought since all of them would be leaving on Monday. And then she would leave less than a week later.

Less than a week.

Boy, how time flies when you're having fun, she thought. And she was having fun. Returning to Waco didn't have the appeal it once did. She had bonded with Chester and the men who worked for Clint, and she thought he had a very special family. They were so different from hers. Even his father, Corey, and stepmother, Abby, were absolutely wonderful. She could feel the closeness and the love among everyone. Those were two things that her family lacked.

"Alyssa."

Clint had whispered her name in his sleep and she snuggled closer to him. She would miss this. Going to bed with him every night and waking up to his lovemaking each and every morning. But as someone once said, all good things must one day come to an end. Over the week she would prepare for the heartbreak she would encounter the moment Clint drove her away from the ranch to the airport. To prepare for that day she needed to start distancing herself from him and she would do so once his family left and it was just the two of them again. It would be for the best.

Alyssa glanced around the huge ballroom filled with people. Chester had been right. Everyone important from all over Texas was attending the charity benefit to give their financial support to the children's hospital. It was even rumored that the President and First Lady would be making an appearance.

She had to admit that she was rendered speechless when they arrived and Clint introduced her to the host and hostess as his wife. Alyssa figured the reason he had done so was to not cause her any embarrassment later. So far no one had questioned his sudden acquisition of a wife. And a few times when one or two people referred to her as Mrs. Westmoreland, she had to stop from stating that wasn't her name.

Another thing she noticed was that the Westmorelands seemed to run in a pack. All of them were standing together in one spot and it was obvious they were a family. All the men in the family resembled one another in their facial features, height and sex appeal. And the Westmoreland women—sisters, cousins and wives—were all beautiful. They made stunning couples. There were Clint's cousin Jared with his wife, Dana; his cousin Storm with his wife, Jayla; his cousin Spencer and his wife, Chardonnay; his cousin Dare and his wife, Shelly; his cousin Thorn and his wife, Tara; and his cousin Ian and his wife, Brooke.

The group also included Clint's brother Cole, who didn't bother to bring a date; his cousin Reggie, who hadn't brought a date, either; Casey and McKinnon; and Clint's father and stepmother, Corey and Abby Westmoreland. Such an imposing group, she thought, and several times Thorn, who was nationally known for the motorcycles he built and raced, was approached by several people wanting his autograph.

"Did I tell you how beautiful you look tonight?"

Alyssa glanced up at the tall, handsome man who hadn't left her side all evening. She smiled up at him. "Yes, you told me. Thank you," she said.

And if he hadn't, his gaze had said it all when she had walked out of the bathroom after getting dressed. Casey, who had once owned a clothing store, had been instrumental in helping her select a dress, a short, black, clingy number that Casey claimed would hit her brother between the eyes when he saw it. Alyssa wasn't sure whether Clint had gotten hit between the eyes, but it was evident he liked seeing her in the dress. And if she was reading his mind correctly, he was counting the hours until he would get the chance to take it off of her.

"Well, well, look who's here. I can't believe my eyes. What are you doing here, Alyssa?"

Dread settled in the pit of Alyssa's stomach at the sound of that voice. She turned and tried to retain her composure when she not only saw Kim but also Kevin. She shook her head, shocked, not believing they were here tonight, of all places, and together. Kim was plastered to Kevin's side as if she wanted to make it obvious that tonight they were a couple.

Alyssa found her voice to speak. "Kim, Kevin, how are you? It's nice seeing the both of you and I'm here for the same reason you are, to support the children's hospital."

"Like you can afford to do that," Kim said with an obvious sneer, not caring who standing around her was listening. "Aunt Claudine claims you left Waco to go work for a client, but I figure you're still licking your wounds because I took Kevin away from you."

Alyssa knew Kim was deliberately trying to embarrass her in front of everyone and a part of Alyssa wished at that moment she was anywhere but there. Having all her personal business exposed to everyone, especially the Westmorelands, was humiliating.

But then she happened to notice that Clint had moved closer to her side, had placed a protective arm around her waist. And out of the corner of her eye she saw the other Westmorelands closing ranks around her, as well.

"Please introduce me to your friends, Alyssa," Clint said.

Only someone as up close, intimate and personal to Clint as she was would detect the edgy steel in his voice. She glanced up at him. He hadn't taken his gaze off Kim and Kevin, and the look in his eyes matched the tone she had heard in his voice.

She cleared her throat. "Clint, this is Kevin and Kim. Kim and I are cousins. Kevin and Kim, this is Clint Westmoreland," Alyssa said.

It was only then that Clint shifted his gaze back to her and she was aware that already he had figured things out. Kevin was her former fiancé and Kim was the woman who had deliberately slept with him to ruin her wedding day. Kim was also Alyssa's cousin.

Kim, who appreciated a good-looking man when she saw one, smiled sweetly at Clint. "So, you're that client she ran off to work for," she said in a smooth, silky voice as her flirty gaze rake him from head to toe.

Clint smiled at Kim, although anyone knowing him could see the smile didn't quite reach his eyes. "No, I'm not Alyssa's client," he said in a clear and firm voice. "I'm Alyssa's husband."

Fourteen

Alyssa thought for as long as she lived she would never forget the shocked look that appeared on Kim's face with Clint's statement. Kim was dumbstruck. Kevin had also seemed to lose his voice, but had quickly regained it. While Kevin stood there babbling, trying to apologize for Kim's rudeness, Clint had taken Alyssa's hand in his, and he, as well as the other Westmorelands, had walked away leaving Kim and Kevin looking like fools. In the end, the embarrassment had been theirs.

They had returned home a few hours ago. Neither Clint nor any of the other Westmorelands had brought up the incident with Kim and Kevin. Alyssa guessed that before the night was over Clint would talk to her about the ugly scene and the party.

She was already in bed, but Clint, his brother and cousins were engaged in a card game. Although she was tired and sleepy, she was determined to stay awake and talk to him. He deserved to know the entire story as to why Kim disliked her so.... Not that it was an excuse for her cousin's behavior.

Later, Alyssa glanced toward the bedroom door. It opened and Clint walked in. He had removed his jacket and tie, and the two top buttons of his shirt were open. He closed the door behind him and stood leaning against it and stared at her. She knew she owed him an apology. In trying to embarrass her, Kim and Kevin had probably embarrassed him, as well. He hadn't deserved it, just like he didn't deserve the predicament that had placed her here, messing up his life as he knew it.

He didn't say anything. He just continued to stare at her. He hadn't seemed upset with her during the course of the evening but she couldn't help wondering if he'd only held his temper in check around his family, and if now, since they were alone, he would let her know how he really felt.

"Why didn't you tell me the full story?" he finally asked.

Alyssa sighed. There was no need to pretend she didn't understand what he was asking. "At the time I didn't think there was a need, Clint," she said, hoping he understood. "Besides, whenever you spoke of your relatives I could feel the love and warmth all of you shared. It's not that way in my family."

He then moved and came closer to the bed and sat on the edge. "Kim really has issues, doesn't she?"

Alyssa thought that was a nice way of putting it. "Yes. She'd always been the center of attention and when I arrived on the scene it didn't sit well with her. And later when I found out my grandfather was actually my father, then she—"

"Whoa. Back up," he said, interrupting. "What do you mean your grandfather was actually your father?"

Alyssa knew that he deserved to know everything. "On his deathbed, the man who I thought was my grandfather confessed to being my father. Before then I'd always thought I was the illegitimate daughter of his dead son, the one who had been a Texas Ranger and had died in the line of duty."

She paused before continuing. "From what I understand, my grandmother died years ago and my grandfather was a widower who had raised two sons, Todd and Kim's father, Jessie. When Todd was killed, Grandpa was really torn up about it and went out drinking to drown in his sorrows. That's the night he had an affair with my mother. She was working as a waitress at the bar. She told him she had gotten pregnant and he provided for my care. When she sent me to live with him, a decision was made to let everyone think I was Todd's illegitimate daughter. The only person who knew the truth other than Grandpa was Aunt Claudine."

Clint nodded. "What was the reason that your mother gave you up?"

Alyssa sighed again before answering. "Because she found out that her new boyfriend was trying to come on to me."

She saw Clint's face harden at that statement. "And you haven't seen or heard from her since?" he asked.

"No. And according to Aunt Claudine, she never wrote or asked how I was doing. She no longer cared," Alyssa said sadly.

The pain she felt whenever she remembered her mother's denial came back, and she didn't realize tears were in her eyes until Clint reached out and took his fingertip and wiped one away. "This has been one heck of a night for you," he said softly. "Go on and get some rest."

She nodded, still unable to decipher his mood or feelings on what she had told him. Without removing his clothes he stretched out on the bed beside her and held her in his arms. And he stayed there with her until she went to sleep.

Alyssa woke the next morning in bed alone. She couldn't help wondering what the Westmorelands thought of her. Nor could she help wondering what Clint thought of her, as well. This was the first morning, since they'd begun sleeping together, that he hadn't woken her with lovemaking.

That thought remained on her mind while she showered and got dressed. When she opened the door to the hall, Clint was standing against the wall waiting for her. He was dressed in a pair of jeans and a chambray shirt. As usual, he looked great.

"Good morning," he said, smiling at her.

It was a smile that made her insides feel somewhat jittery.

"Good morning, Clint," she said, searching his expression in an attempt to decipher his mood.

"I know you haven't eaten breakfast yet, but I was wondering if you would go riding with me this morning. I promise not to keep you out long."

"Sure," she said and shrugged.

They walked together through the house. The place seemed rather quiet, especially for a house full of guests. It was after eight in the morning. She had discovered over the past few days that the Westmorelands were early risers.

"Where's everyone?"

"Sleeping in late, I guess," Clint said.

"Oh."

When they walked outside she saw two horses were saddled and ready for them. Clint helped her mount Sunshine, the docile mare he had given her to ride, and then he mounted Royal. She glanced over at him.

"Where are we going?"

"To the south ridge," he said mysteriously.

She nodded. They hadn't ridden on that part of his property in a while. Thanks to Clint she felt comfortable riding and appreciated the slow pace he set for them. They rode in silence, enjoying the beautiful morning.

They had been riding for a while when Clint finally brought the horses to a stop. "This is a nice place to stop," he said, glancing over at her.

For what? she couldn't help wondering. *Was he going to ask her to leave the ranch? Had he figured out that the best way to end their farce of a marriage and quickly was to forget the annulment and file for a quick divorce instead?*

She watched as Clint dismounted from Royal and tied him to a tree before coming back to help her off of Sunshine. He tied Sunshine to a tree, as well.

"Come on," Clint said, reaching for her hand. "Let's take a walk so we can talk."

She pulled her hand back. "Talking isn't necessary. I know what you want."

His brows drew together. "Do you?"

"Yes, I do," she said.

"And what do you think I want?" he asked, leaning against an oak tree.

She glanced around instead of looking at him and then she brought her gaze back to his.

"You want to skip the annulment and go straight to a divorce," Alyssa said.

Clint could only stare at her. What she had said was so far from the truth it was pitiful. What had happened last night at the ball had been an eye-opener for him. When Kim had said those insulting remarks his protective instincts had kicked in. He had immediately wanted to shield her from any kind of hurt, harm or danger.

Something else had also kicked in. His heart. He realized at that moment how much he cared for her. He loved her. And he wanted to always be by her side to protect her from the Kims and Kevins of the world. For him it wasn't a matter of lust, as he had first assumed. He realized now that his feelings for Alyssa were a matter of love. He couldn't imagine her leaving him or the ranch next week. He had no intentions of letting her go and the sooner she knew it the better.

"There will be no divorce, Alyssa. And there won't be an annulment," he said as he took a step toward her.

"What are you saying?"

A smile touched his lips and he reached into his back pocket and pulled out a small box and opened it. There was a beautiful wedding ring in the box.

"I'm saying that what I want is to marry you all over again. Make it truly right this time. Since the laws of Texas declare we're already man and wife, let's make it real. Let's renew our vows," he said.

He then got down on one knee and glanced up at her.

"Alyssa, will you continue to be my wife, till death us do part?"

Alyssa was shocked speechless. Tears flooded her eyes. She shook her head and tried wiping the tears away with her hand—the one Clint wasn't slipping the ring onto.

"But—but you can't want to stay married to me. You don't love me," she said.

Satisfied the ring was a perfect fit, Clint stood and smiled at her.

"Now that's where you're wrong. I do love you. I think I fell in love with you the first time we played our own special game," he said.

"Oh, Clint," she said, smiling through her tears.

He pulled her into his arms and murmured against her ear, "Is that a yes?"

She pulled back and smiled up at him. "That's definitely a yes! Oh, Clint, I will marry you again," she said.

"Thank you, sweetheart," he said. And then he was lowering his mouth to hers while pulling her closer into his arms. The kiss was long, deep and passionate. Clint knew that it wasn't enough, but he broke the kiss off anyway. He knew there was something else he had to tell her.

"You know when we left the ranch and you asked where everyone was?" he asked her.

She nodded. "You told me they were probably sleeping in," she said.

"I lied."

Alyssa lifted a brow. "They aren't sleeping in?"

"No."

A confused looked touched her features. "Where are they?"

"In the barn getting things ready."

He could tell by her expression that now she was really confused so he decided to explain things. "I told everyone last night that I planned to ask you to marry me today. Abby suggested that while we had everyone here, we might as well renew our vows today. We can always have a reception for the rest of the family later, preferably on my father's mountain in Montana when the weather gets warm," he said.

Alyssa truly didn't know what to say at first.

"Your family is doing that for me?"

Clint smiled. "They are doing it for us. They know how much I love you. I think they realized it before I did because all of them, with the exception of Cole and Reggie, have been there, done that. They know what it is like to fall in love with your heart even when your mind is still in denial," he said.

He leaned down and kissed her again and when she wrapped her arms around his neck and returned the kiss, he knew that when they married this time around, it would be forever.

Epilogue

"You tricked me," Alyssa said.

She looked at herself in the full-length mirror before turning around and giving Casey an all-accusing look.

Casey laughed. "I did not. I just know my brother and figured he would get around to popping the question sooner or later. I just thought you should be prepared when he did. Like I said, he's slow. And since we were going shopping that day, I figured you might as well purchase a second dress just in case."

Alyssa shook her head. She had tried on several outfits for the ball and Casey had convinced her to buy the two she liked the best instead of just one. Now it seemed the second outfit, a beautiful off-white tea-length gown, would be the one she would marry Clint in. She had to admit that it was simply perfect.

"You look beautiful, Alyssa," Aunt Claudine said from across the room.

"Thanks, Aunt Claudine," Alyssa said lovingly to her aunt.

Her aunt's arrival had been another surprise the Westmorelands had sprung on her. They had contacted Claudine the night before and made arrangements for the older woman to fly in for today's festivities.

Alyssa still couldn't believe what the Westmorelands had accomplished in a single night. When she had been in her bedroom wondering how they felt about her after that embarrassing fiasco with Kim and Kevin, they'd huddled together somewhere with Clint and planned the ceremony for today. They were determined to make her one of them. And in her heart, she knew her marriage today would be more than just a renewing of her and Clint's vows. The marriage ceremony would affirm her love for Clint, but it would also proclaim her membership in the Westmoreland clan.

Tara Westmoreland glanced at her watch. "It's about time for you to make an entrance," she said, smiling. "The last thing you want to do is to keep a Westmoreland man waiting on his wedding day."

Alyssa smiled as she glanced around at all the women in the room. Westmoreland women, all of them, except for her aunt. "Thanks for everything. I already feel blessed having all of you in my life," Alyssa said. She had a feeling they knew what she meant.

"There're a few more where we came from," Shelly Westmoreland spoke up. "And they're all dying to meet you and send their love and regrets that they can't be here. We plan to have a reception on Corey's Mountain. With the exception of Delaney and Casey, we ladies became Westmorelands through marriage. What we discovered is a sisterhood that's very special and we welcome you with love."

Tears filled Alyssa's eyes. She was finally getting a family who would love her as much as she loved them.

Thirty minutes later, Alyssa was walking across the span of the room to where Clint, dressed in a dark suit, was standing beside his brother and father. She had asked Chester to give her away and he had truly seemed honored to do so. Casey was her matron of honor.

When she reached Clint, he smiled as he took her hand in his. She smiled back and together they faced the minister. Alyssa knew this was a new beginning for her and she would have a lot to tell her grandkids one day about how she was able to tame the wild and elusive heart of Clint Westmoreland.

* * * * *

COMING NEXT MONTH

#1855 MISTRESS & A MILLION DOLLARS—
Maxine Sullivan
Diamonds Down Under
He will stop at nothing to get what he wants. And if it costs him a million dollars to make her his mistress...so be it!

#1856 IRON COWBOY—Diana Palmer
Long, Tall Texans
He was as ornery as they come. But this billionaire Texan didn't stand a chance of escaping the one woman who was his match... in every way.

#1857 BARGAINING FOR KING'S BABY—Maureen Child
Kings of California
He agreed to marry his rival's daughter to settle a business deal... but she has her own bargain for her soon-to-be husband. Give her a baby or lose the contract!

#1858 THE SPANISH ARISTOCRAT'S WOMAN—
Katherine Garbera
Sons of Privilege
She was only supposed to play the count's lover for one day. But suddenly, she's become his wife.

#1859 CEO'S MARRIAGE SEDUCTION—Anna DePalo
It was the perfect plan. Wed her father's business protégé and have the baby she's been dreaming about...until scandals threaten her plan for the perfect marriage of convenience.

#1860 FOR BLACKMAIL...OR PLEASURE—Robyn Grady
Blackmailing his ex-fiancée into working for him was easy. Denying the attraction still between them could prove to be lethal.

SDCNM0208